My Mother's Gift
Susan B. Roara

Printed in the United States of America
Edited, formatted, and interior design by Kristen Corrects, Inc.
Cover art design by Susan B. Roara

First edition published 2015
10 9 8 7 6 5 4 3 2 1

Roara, Susan B.
My mother's gift / Susan B. Roara
p. cm.
ISBN-13: 978-0-9967822-3-4
ISBN-10: 0996782230

Table of Contents

For Mae, Amelia, Anna, and Jack

With love.

CHAPTER 1

Lucy

There was something about death that I found peaceful, like when you watch a caterpillar transform into a butterfly. The sudden release of its cocooned body, giving way to freedom and flight. The carefree life of the butterfly, floating from flower to flower, landing here and there on some unexpected object or another. That was how I felt about death; I felt we were given the freedom to soar. Still, some souls failed to soar. Some souls screamed as if they had more to say, more to do, as if they weren't finished hiding in their cocoon yet. All I wanted for my family was to feel liberated, my mother, at peace and free from her life. She, however, had different plans for me.

She was screaming and I was listening.

I lay in my bed and I waited for it. It had been one month since my mother's passing and she hadn't missed a day yet. I tried to force myself to sleep but I always grew anxious due to the anticipation. At first, I thought I was imagining things. At first, it was just the ladybug.

It occurred to me that the minor coincidences happened every day; somehow the ladybug would appear on me suddenly and at the strangest of moments. Bizarre instances, when I felt the most hopeless and restless, the ladybug would arrive and land on my eyelash or perhaps my earlobe. I would talk to it lightheartedly. I felt like she was watching over me. I couldn't help but laugh and I was careful not to harm her. I talked to her constantly, asking her for guidance and advice. I convinced myself that it was like prayer. I guess it felt good to talk, even though I thought no one was listening—let alone a ladybug.

Then it happened. I had this preconceived idea in my head that ghosts were cartoon animations meant for children and entertainment. TV images of spirits floating around through the air and images of the dead dominated my predisposed senses. Of course, being haunted wasn't even remotely like that. It was more like a feeling in the air, a strong intuitive image in my mind, and a conscious awareness that something was happening, something greater than me.

I would wake in the night and I would feel her. I would feel her as she touched me delicately on my face. Groggy from my sleep, I would shake it off and tell myself that it was nothing. But, whatever it was, it was enough to wake me from my bedtime, my feelings exhilarated yet relaxed. A peaceful smile would spread across my face, knowing she was here for me, she had chosen me specifically. I was unafraid and curious.

It happened every night at the same time. I knew in my heart what it was. The signs had already been there and when I finally acknowledged her, it grew even more intense.

My mother.

She would softly place her absent finger on my forehead and trail it down until she reached the tip of my nose. I would wake quickly and abruptly, sitting alert in my bed. I would look around the room to see if I could see her ghostly image. I knew she was there with me. At first I wasn't sure, but then I was convinced.

I lay now trying to sleep. She won't come unless I'm sleeping. I'm not sure what this means or why she has chosen me.

I asked my siblings, "Has anyone received any signs from Mom?"

They looked at me confused.

"What kind of signs?" Jessica asked.

9

"Oh, I don't know. Do you feel like she's around you? Her spirit?"

"You're weird, Lucy," Jessica stated, her face scrunched up like a pug's.

"It's not weird. It's like praying to Jesus. He's always around us, except it's Mom," I explained.

"I don't know what you're talking about," Kaylan stated, puzzled, as she continued to look over her summer reading.

"Forget it. Never mind then."

I felt tired now. I looked at the clock; she would be here soon. I closed my eyes and opened my arms as I lay in my bed. I felt the heavy sensation take over me. The warm cozy feeling you get right before your body drifts off into unconsciousness. My brain released control over my body and I fell asleep. I was finally asleep.

CHAPTER 2

Jack

Time seemed to be dragging by. My days were filled with hard work and focus but my nights were difficult. I often walked around the barnyard, looking for additional chores to do, consciously trying to fill the void of an inadequate social life and my need for Lucy. Punishing myself and withholding joy purposely while Lucy and her family mourned their mother. I prayed for her. I prayed for myself. I needed patience, but I had none. I had waited so long. I loved her so much but yet she still remained far and out of my reach.

I sat on the porch swing while I watched the sun set, the moon making its subtle presence into the dimming sky. I loved this time of night. I could feel the breeze of the warm summer air against my face. I could see the lightning bugs start to flicker in

11

the tall grass along the fences. The air smelled sweet, like fresh-cut grass; the horses lingered along the fence line, somehow aware that this time of night was special.

I thought about Lucy and our time together. She would be happy on the farm; I know somehow this was where she should be. We took advantage of our brief moments alone in Connecticut. We walked for hours along the river, holding hands and dreaming of what our life could be like. She talked about her mother, sorrow and regret still fresh and visible on her expression and in her tone. I was proud of her. I was proud of the person that she became, her values much like mine, her need to care for her family—admirable.

We walked and talked about our childhood. "Lucy, remember that time when we were young, when we witnessed the best, most exciting bike race of all time? The time when Charles and a bunch of the fellas were racing their dirt bikes for money?" I watched her expression change into a deep and thoughtful smile.

"How could I forget? That was so exciting, Jack. I remember how protective you were over me, how you didn't want us to get hurt." Lucy wrapped her arm around my waist while we walked. "I was in so much trouble with Thomas after that day; he was so angry with me." Lucy laughed as we talked about the old times. I was happy to make her smile.

I sat on my porch swing, recalling my time with Lucy and the childhood memory of my brother Charles. I thought about Lucy, how I loved her even back then, how I wasn't even aware of how important she was to me. I smiled as I thought about them; I wished I could go back in time, just for a little while, just to remember.

"Jack!" Charles yelled from the hallway of their small ranch-style home.

"I'm coming, Charles! Give me a second!" I replied angrily, annoyed with my brother's insistence. I was busy looking at the newest and greatest dirty magazine my mother's current boyfriend left in the bathroom. I was thirteen and just starting to take a notice in girls. My brother Charles seemed far more interested in his dirt bike and skateboard to care.

Charles bounded into the bedroom, full of energy and enthusiasm. "What is taking so long, Jack?"

"Take a look at this, Charles!" I shoved the dirty magazine in Charles' face.

"Wow! Where did you get that?" Charles asked, looking around him.

"In the bathroom!"

"Quick, roll it up and shove it under your mattress." I did what I was told. Charles grabbed me by the arm and helped me to my feet. "Come on, Jack. The guys are waiting for us at the pond."

"What's going on?"

"That piece of garbage Josh Jenkins wants to race. He told Lucy to get us up to the pond and if we didn't show up, he was going to tell everyone that we're chicken shit!" Charles paced the room.

"Is Lucy going?" The mention of Lucy's name suddenly made me more interested in my brother's plight.

"I don't know, who cares!" Charles threw his arms up in the air.

I cared. I was becoming very fond and very aware of Lucy. Lucy was sweet and pretty. Her big eyes were a deep blue, her eyelashes thick and dark…and then her smile. She had the best smile, her face always cheerful and pleasant. She was easy on my eyes, yet she could run and jump and play just like any of my other friends. Her mother showed an interest in my brother and me and it felt good to be cared about. Lucy's mother displayed a concern that made me feel special. I tried my best to be well behaved when I was around Lucy and her family.

"Come *on*, Jack!"

"Okay, okay. I'm coming!" Do you have gas for that stupid bike?" I asked as I stood and walked toward Charles.

"Yup, all set. Hurry up!"

"Let me grab a helmet at least," I stated. "I hope your bike is as good as you think it is, buddy. I hope it doesn't do that thing…you know…break down." I laughed as I slapped Charles on his back. The two of us walked out of our house to the driveway. Charles hopped on his bike.

"Shut up and jump on," Charles yelled, grinning mischievously.

I jumped on the back of the dirt bike and Charles raced down the street toward the pond. Five minutes later, we arrived and as we approached the small crowd, I noticed only one thing: Lucy was not there. I felt instantly disappointed. Charles stopped and revved his bike a few times while I jumped off, scanning over the crowd of boys, looking for Josh. Charles approached him first but I was two feet behind him, my arms crossed, my face focused in a stare-down of masculine worth.

"What the hell are you doing up here, Josh? These are our woods! Don't you have some other playground you could drag that stupid, ugly dirt bike through?" Charles yelled.

I knew Charles was very proud of his dirt bike. It was the only thing he took care of. The only thing he cared about besides me.

"Ha! Look at your bike! I don't think you have one original part on the whole thing," Josh said, pointing and laughing. Josh's bike was much newer and nicer than Charles'. Josh's father had a great job, they had a big house and his mother was the local charity worker for the church and school. Josh was a spoiled rotten boy who got everything he wanted. His bike was much nicer, but I knew one thing: Josh couldn't ride to save his life.

"Well, I guess we'll find out what's what, won't we, Josh?" Charles started his bike with a quick jump and fell into place at the imaginary starting line. Josh circled his bike around the same way and the two were head to head at the beginning of the bike trail.

The neighborhood kids ran to stand watch at the lookout points along the trail. It was early enough in the morning and the summer heat hadn't made it uncomfortable yet. The woods were cool and shaded and you could hear the stream from the waterfalls in the distance.

Charles was yelling over the sound of the motorbike engines. He and Josh were making a wager. My eyes went wide when I heard my brother state, "ONE HUNDRED DOLLARS" to the winner. I watched Josh as he looked around, worry evident on his face while he shook Charles' hand, sealing the deal. Just as the race was about to begin, I saw out of the corner of my eye Lucy and her younger sister Jessica walking hand-in-hand up the battered parking lot. I felt the smile spread brightly across my face as I waved to Lucy, hurrying her along so she didn't miss anything.

"Luce! You need to hurry and stay out of the way," I warned.

Lucy dragged her sister quickly and caught up to me, and we began to jog down a side path into the woods to secure a spot on the trail, the sound of the revving bikes becoming a little more distant. As we ran, we could hear one of the boys start to count down: "FIVE, FOUR, THREE, TWO…ONE! GO!" The race was on.

"Watch your step. Grab my hand, Lucy. Climb up that rock. Do you have it?"

"Yes. Can you help Jessica?"

"Come here, Jess. Place your foot on my hand. I'm going to lift you up on the rock."

"Okay, Jack," Jessica stated in her small voice. I lifted her little light body with ease and the three of us stood tall on the large boulder nestled into the woods along the path. We could hear the motorbikes and some of the kids hooting and hollering, but we couldn't see anything yet.

"What's happening, Jack?" Lucy asked.

"Charles made a crazy bet. A hundred dollars if he wins the race!"

"ONE HUNDRED DOLLARS! Your momma is going to whoop you boys," Jessica stated with her hands on her hips.

"Shush, Jess, you be quiet or I'll bring you back home," Lucy scolded her. "Jack, where will he get that kind of money?" she asked, concerned.

I winked at her with confidence. "Don't worry, Lucy. Charles isn't going to lose. Josh is going to have to worry about where he's going to find that kind of money. He's going to have to ask his daddy for it."

Just then, the motorbikes came roaring down around the corner. The last leg of the trail was very rugged with boulders and tree roots. I instinctively stood in front of Jessica and Lucy with my arms stretched out in front of them, protecting them from rock, dust, and dirt but impairing their vision of the most important thing, the race. Lucy stood on her tippy toes so that she could see the trail over my arms while Jessica kneeled down under them so that she could see, just the same. I laughed as I teased them, tickling little Jessica in the process.

Finally, Charles came thundering past us, in the lead and not letting up one bit. The three of us jumped and hollered with excitement, cheering and encouraging Charles to the finish. Charles threw his fist into the air, a proud and clear indication that he intended to win. Lucy and I high-fived each other and then I lifted little Jessica high into the sky as she screamed, "Did you see that, Jack? He's going to win! He's going to win!"

We watched as Josh finally passed us up the hill, in last place. I jumped down and helped Jessica and Lucy off the rock and then the three of us ran up the path to meet with the others at the finish line.

When we arrived, Charles was off his bike and little skinny Jimmy Daniels was slapping him on the back, congratulating him. I stared at my brother, proud and impressed.

"I get half!" I joked, then congratulated my brother.

"You are one lucky son of a bitch, Chucky boy!" Jimmy said.

"Hey Charles!" Josh yelled from his bike, heading out of the parking lot. "I've got more money in my little tiny piggy bank than you do in this whole entire world."

"Good, Josh! Then you shouldn't feel so bad when you fork over the one hundred dollars. I want it within the hour!" Josh flipped Charles the bird and then sped off down the road.

Lucy grabbed Jessica's hand and they began to make their way back home.

"Hey Lucy, wait up," I yelled.

She slowed down briefly until I reached them. "I've got to get Jessica home, Jack. I'm not sure where Thomas is and I really don't want him to find us here."

"Okay, Lucy. I get it," I said. I knew Thomas well and I knew that it was a bad idea for the girls to get caught up in something Thomas would consider "inappropriate" for his sisters. "Well, when can I see you again?" I asked. I watched Lucy carefully. I watched her as she raised her eyes to mine; her cheeks were rosy and her sudden bashfulness, adorable.

Lucy shrugged her shoulders. "Anytime, Jack."

"I'll stop by later then. Maybe we can hang out?"

"Sure." She smiled. "I'll be home."

Sitting on my porch swing, I remembered watching Lucy take her sister's hand, making their way up the street. I remembered being so envious of them and thinking how lucky they were to be a part of a loving family, to have a father and a normal mother.

I stared into the night sky enjoying the summer air and reminiscing about the past, about Lucy and my brother. I was ashamed of how I felt. I realized suddenly that I wanted Lucy to pick me. I tried so hard to understand her choices, to respect them, but I knew deep down that I wanted her to choose me, not her family. It was a selfish thought, I recognized, but I was angry and lonely.

I noticed a set of car lights making their way up the driveway. I looked down at my watch; it was a little late for

21

visitors. I watched as the car pulled in and I was surprised to see that it was Angie. We hadn't spoken much since I returned from Connecticut. I wasn't sure how I felt about her and I certainly didn't want to lead her on.

Angie exited her car and approached the porch casually, an innocent yet knowing smile on her face. "Hey Jack," she said pleasantly.

"Hi Ang.... What are you doing out this time of night?" I asked curiously. I watched Angie stop briefly in the driveway as she showed attention to one of the barn cats calmly circling her ankles. Angie climbed the porch steps and leaned delicately against the railings, a folder in her hand.

"I was driving by and I saw that you had the porch lights on. I hope it's not too late."

"No, not at all. Please, sit down." I moved over to make room for Angie on the porch swing.

"I wanted to bring you something." Angie reached into her folder and pulled out a picture.

She showed it to me. It was a picture of my teammates and me at our last game. Lionel was squeezing his arms around me, while another player was reaching to hit my helmet as we celebrated, our mouths opened as we yelled, our eyes searching for each other as we experienced the roar of the crowd and unbelievable joy of our victory.

"Wow!" I exclaimed. "Where did you get this?"

"I took it the night of the game. I took a bunch of pictures, but this one was truly the best. I love your expression. I think I was in the right place at the right time. I can still feel the joy of the moment when I look at this picture of you. I took it right after you realized you had won the game."

"This is really special, Angie. Thank you so much. I had no idea you were taking pictures." That day was filled with so many surprises, so many distractions, that I vaguely remember the celebration. Seeing this picture took me back to that special moment, the moment of our victory.

"It's just a hobby really, but I enjoy photography." Angie stood to move off the porch.

"Where are you going?" I asked.

Angie shrugged her shoulders. "I was just driving by and I wanted to give that to you."

I stood and approached Angie while she tried to turn to leave.

"Stay. I'll grab us some beers and we can talk." I stared at Angie. I was so unsure.

"Yeah, okay, Jack. I would like that." She gave a lopsided smile.

I walked into the kitchen and opened the refrigerator. I felt the nervous guilt weighing heavily on my shoulders. This was no big deal.

What harm could it cause?

CHAPTER 3

Lucy

The weeks after my mother's death were a blur. Jack left for Indiana. I knew deep down that we may never see each other again, but I was hopeful. Our time together seemed like a dream, like perhaps I had imagined the whole thing. At times I cried myself to sleep at night, feeling totally helpless and lost to my emotions. I felt guilty and fearful that I was spending too much thought and energy on Jack and not enough time grieving the loss of my mother. I wanted so badly to move forward, but it was difficult. The loss of my mother was painful, the loss I felt for Jack heart-wrenching. I felt that I fulfilled my purpose; I felt that we were meant to find Jack and we did. Our connection was powerful and I hoped and prayed that he would wait for me, that we might be together when our lives were less complicated. I had graduated high school and the summer was upon us in full speed.

My intentions were good: I wanted to support my father, help my siblings, and get through the summer with some sort of normalcy.

I imagined that I had enough strength to assist my family as we worked through the loss of my mother and the parental void we all felt within our house. I hoped that I could fill in the blanks, be caring and encouraging, kind and helpful. I believed in my sense of responsibility, my sense that we should be taking care of each other now, the matriarchal family, disrupted. I knew my siblings needed me and it gave me courage—to be needed.

Julia was busy commuting back and forth to school. Kathryn and Charles had decided to charter a boat for the summer in Boston—an exciting career endeavor, as they wanted to explore the world of commercial fishing. Thomas had vowed to spend every last minute of his summer with Amelia. I had decided to make this summer as special as I could for Kaylan, Jessica, and Mikey.

My father was having a difficult time coming to terms with my mother's death. He disappeared into his garage whenever he could, coming out occasionally for meals and work. I tried to talk to him, using unforceful tactics to encourage him to open up to me. He was devastated over my mother. I knew that he needed time to mourn and I hoped that if we gave him enough time, then perhaps he would eventually come around. We still needed him. He still needed to be our father.

Every day felt the same. I woke in the morning and counted down the hours until the evening. Keeping busy in between, hoping for some joy along the way. The routine was monotonous. Wake, cook, clean, bathe, sleep. It felt mundane, but it made our lives normal for now. I tried to stick to the same routine as my mother had. It brought comfort throughout our days and my siblings unknowingly benefitted from it.

It was an early morning; I made a pot of coffee and lunch for my father. He had been working harder than ever. Like me, my father thought it was easier to stay busy. Your day moved faster and you didn't give yourself any time to grieve or think about her.

I grabbed a cup of coffee and sat at the kitchen counter, enjoying the short-lived peace of the morning when I heard the car door slam. I looked out of the window and was surprised to see that it was my grandmother. A visit at this hour in the morning felt uneasy, like we were about to engage in something unfortunate. I reluctantly opened the door to greet her and to let her in. Her smile was nervous and full of ulterior motives.

"Hey, Gram. What are you doing here this early?" I asked, concerned as she pushed past me, entering our kitchen.

"I came to talk to your father. Is he home?" she asked. I looked over at Kaylan, who had slowly made her way down the stairs, dazed from sleep and annoyed by the noisy conversation. My grandmother was never a quiet woman; perhaps it was her stubborn refusal to wear hearing aids, but for whatever reason, she was a loud speaker.

"Yeah, he's upstairs." I approached Kaylan quietly. "Kaylan? Can you run and tell Dad that Grandma's here?" I asked in a semi-whisper.

"Sure!" Kaylan replied loudly. "Dad! Grandma's here!" Kaylan screamed obnoxiously from her chair.

"Kaylan, you don't have to yell," I said, irritated. "Walk upstairs and tell Dad that Grandma is here. It's unpleasant," I lectured.

Kaylan turned and stomped up the stairs to talk to my father.

My grandmother looked at me, eager to speak, her face wrinkled with concern and worry. "How are you doing, Lucy? With your mother gone?"

I looked at her thoughtfully. How does she think we're doing? "It's hard, Gram. Everywhere I go, I picture her. I miss her."

My grandmother nodded her head.

"Can I get you some tea, Gram?" I asked as I moved across the kitchen.

"Sure, Lucy, that would be wonderful." She settled in at the kitchen counter.

I placed the kettle on the stove and set out two coffee mugs. "Flavored or regular?" I asked. Kaylan returned to the kitchen and took her seat.

"I'll have regular, dear."

I stood at the stove and waited for the kettle to boil. I could hear the shower running. "Dad must be in the shower. I'm sure he'll come down when he's through."

"I came here to check on you girls. I know it hasn't been easy. I want to help you."

I turned to look at my grandmother. Her hair was neatly washed and styled, her makeup simple yet bright. But her eyes—her eyes were unsettled. She looked all over the kitchen, up the cabinets, down to the floors, everywhere but in my face. Her nervous posture was obvious, her intentions questionable.

"Thank you, Gram, but I think we're getting along."

Why does a teakettle take so long to boil? I glanced over at my grandmother as she waited patiently for her tea. I smiled weakly at her as the kitchen became thick with silence.

Julia walked in suddenly, confused by the amount of social activity within the house. "Hey, Gram. I'm surprised to see you here," she stated sleepily. Julia glanced over at Kaylan, who was quietly observing the morning commotion. Julia threw her arm around Kaylan's shoulders, giving her a quick hug. "How did you sleep, Kay? Why are *you* up so early?"

Kaylan pushed Julia away from her, laughing. "I had a weird dream."

Julia glanced at her again, concern etched over her forehead as she asked, "Are you alright?"

Kaylan hopped off the chair and headed toward the family room. "I'm fine," she stated flippantly. "I'm going to watch TV. Call me if you need me."

Julia looked over at me as we exchanged a shared concern over our sibling's sleeping habits, or lack thereof. Julia continued to make herself a cup of tea and joined my grandmother at the counter. "So Gram, how are you? What brings you by this morning? Is everything alright?"

"Oh, I just came by to check on you kids," she answered.

I was grateful for Julia's appearance and for her astute observance of the situation. Two against one seemed likely better odds than one against one. I hadn't noticed the suitcase on the floor next to my grandmother, but of course, Julia did.

"Why the suitcase?" she asked suspiciously.

My grandmother looked down at the ground where her suitcase sat, watching Julia tap it gently with her shoeless foot.

"I thought it would be a good idea if I stayed awhile, with you kids. I think it's what your mother would want," she replied with unnecessary confidence.

Julia looked at me with wide eyes.

"Where would you stay, Gram? We don't have a spare bedroom," I asked nervously. Having my grandmother staying at the house would be like living in a bad dream; with all the unwanted rules and regulations that she was sure to impose on us kids, it would feel foreign and invasive. My ideas of having a fun-filled summer would have ceased to exist if my grandmother had her way. Besides, we weren't babies. Mikey and Jessica were in middle school and Kaylan was heading into her freshman year at high school.

"Gram, really. I think it's unnecessary. We're managing just fine. I'll be coming home occasionally and Lucy is more than capable of handling the house and kids. And Dad's here!" Julia expressed confidently.

"You kids deserve more. Lucy deserves to start focusing on her own life, not sitting around here acting like a parent. I think it's best if I stay for few days and see for myself. I need to know that you children are being cared for by your father." My grandmother stood from her stool and walked around the counter to the sink and started to tidy up the kitchen. She acted as if the decision had been made, like she was no longer a guest sipping tea at the counter; she was now in charge. It was an unsaid assumption in our household; the person who held the unwanted position behind the sink surely was one who held an authoritative role within the family. I wanted to put my mother's apron on and shove her out of my way.

I turned to face the counter and to grab some sugar as I thought to myself, *Dad is going to be pissed. Does she think this is going to be that easy?*

My father walked down the stairs. "Hello, Frances," he said dryly.

My grandmother approached him casually and gave my father a quick kiss and hug.

"Hello, Joe."

"What brings you by?" My father grabbed himself a cup of coffee.

My grandmother gathered herself some courage and abruptly revealed her plan to my father, her plan to move in for a week or so.

My father blinked his eyes twice. He choked on his coffee and swallowed hard, trying not to shower us with his first sip of the day. He stared at her and waited. He waited for the joke to be over.

"I'm serious, Joe. I'm sure you could use another hand around here. All this responsibility shouldn't fall on your children," my grandmother lectured.

My father started to laugh and shook his head. "You're unbelievable," he said angrily. He began to pace the kitchen; back and forth he walked with no certain purpose. "You had your chance to care for your own daughter, my *wife*. How did that work out for us, Frances?" My father glared at my grandmother while he spoke to her with dripping distaste. My father would never forgive my grandmother for the lack of urgency in her attitude toward caring for my mother. My grandmother's denial over the existence of my mother's mental problems, her lack of acceptance over the reasons why my mother struggled so, didn't sit well with my father.

"Joe, please don't raise your voice in front of the girls. I've only come here to help. Not to start trouble." My grandmother moved around my father and grabbed a tissue out of her coat pocket and began to dab at her tearful eyes. Her voice shook and trembled while she confronted him. I looked at Julia. Julia seemed cool and collected while she leaned back on the counter watching the event unfold. My father stood and slammed his fists onto the counter.

"You are a self-servicing, self-absorbed bitch, Frances. You're only here so that you could feel better about yourself. You've made your own mistakes in raising your children; *you* need to deal with them! We aren't here to help you lift the burden of guilt that you feel over losing your daughter. I wouldn't allow my children to spend one day in this house with you. These are my children and I'll handle them however I see fit. You've had your chances." My father stood tall in the kitchen, his presence intimidating. He angrily tossed his coffee mug into the sink, the remnants of the coffee splattering over the basin and counters. He took a deep breath and tried to compose himself.

"Now, if you would excuse me, I need to go to work. Julia, make sure your grandmother finds her way out of this house before I return." My father turned and grabbed his lunchbox and walked out of the door, slamming it behind him.

I stood there watching my grandmother cry, shocked at my father's anger. I knew my father was furious about my mother, but there seemed to be more to this story. I walked over to my grandmother and put my arm around her, to comfort her.

"I apologize, girls. I shouldn't have come so soon," my grandmother said through her tears.

"It's okay, Gram. I don't know why Dad is so mad. Maybe it's best we give him some time," Julia stated.

"I feel so lonely. I'm so deeply hurt over your mother's passing. Maybe your father's right. Maybe it is my fault." My grandmother stopped to blow her nose into her tissue. I walked over to the counter and grabbed the Kleenex box and handed it to her.

"Don't blame yourself, Gram. Everything happened so quickly. I don't think any one of us could have seen what would happen next. It was all so devastating," Julia said with patience.

My grandmother gathered her composure and stood to give Julia and me a hug. "You don't know how it feels, to be a mother. You will someday."

"Let me grab your bag for you, Gram," I replied.

"Thank you, Lucy."

Julia and I walked my grandmother to her car and I placed her bag into the trunk.

"Please, girls, call me," she begged.

"We will, Gram. We'll keep you posted and if we need you, we promise we will call," I said, trying to comfort her.

"Okay," she replied as she got into her car, tears still gathered in her eyes.

"Bye, Gram." Julia waved as she pulled out of the driveway.

Julia and I stood there in the front yard shaking our heads. "She'll never come back here," I said matter-of-factly.

"Nor should she." Julia turned and walked back into the house. I watched her as she retreated to the kitchen. *That was an odd thing to say*, I thought to myself.

CHAPTER 4

Lucy

I managed to make dinner, clean up, and get the kids settled to bed in record time. My father called earlier to tell me he would be working a double shift and not to wait for him. Oddly enough, I already knew this. I walked into my bedroom and plopped myself onto my bed. I looked forward to having a quiet moment in hopes that I could communicate with my mother. My brain was constantly bombarded with images and thoughts that I didn't quite understand. Visions, I would say. They were becoming more pronounced, more vivid and random. Moments when my brain seemed to be at rest, the thoughts would come. I could say that it was just my imagination getting the best of me, but the visions seemed to have a purpose, a story to tell.

I sat on my bed and closed my eyes. The image of the young girl appeared in my head again. I thought about her and how her face had haunted me, unexpectedly, throughout my day. I couldn't quite see her, but I could tell that she was five or six years old. I shook my head to clear the image. I stood, changed into my pajamas, and climbed into my bed, exhausted. I prayed like I did every night. I prayed for my father. I prayed for my siblings. I asked my mother to look over our family. I closed my eyes and I waited. I waited for sleep.

My nighttime routine had been consistently disruptive and restless since my mother passed. The abrupt awakening I endured every night by her touch and then the dreams. My daytime routine, also disrupted by the bizarre images and messages I didn't quite understand. The stress and worry over Jack and the sleeplessness was starting to take a toll on me.

This night, the nightmares began.

I dreamt that I was walking down a dark and long hallway. I could see doors upon doors lining the walls of the walkway, but I couldn't quite manage to open any of them. I felt frightened but I didn't know why. When I reached the end of the hallway, an entrance appeared and revealed a small bedroom with a small bed. I saw her, the child. She lied on the bed facing the wall. I was unable to see her face. She did not move.

I recognized the room. It was my bedroom at my great grandmother's farm. I looked around the clouded area, darkness overshadowing the once bright and cheerful light of the familiar space. I felt tall in the room, like the ceiling and walls were starting to close around me. The bedroom contained a small bed and nightstand, a small dresser and a closet. One window casted a shadowy light into the room as I tried to squint and focus on seeing the small child.

I tried to talk to her, but as in many of my dreams, I had no voice. My mouth and lips would move, but nothing would escape them. I tried to reach out and touch her, but her bed moved farther and farther away from my hand. I heard someone. I heard a man. Invisible daggers rained fear into my heart as this man's voice sent my core racing into a panic. His footsteps echoed as he creaked his way down the hallway. He called her name.

"Sarah?" he sang softly. "Where are you?" he asked in a creepy, falsely kind voice.

My urge was to slam the door shut and lock it. I turned and tried to close the door. I used all of my strength, but the door wouldn't budge. I looked back at the child, Sarah. She lay very still. She seemed unafraid—or was she sleeping? I wasn't sure. I knew this man was bad. He wanted to hurt Sarah. I felt it in my

40

chest and in my soul. I could see him coming, his blurry image frightening. His face was dangerously bizarre, his mouth and nose like a dog's face, his teeth big and jagged and sharp looking. His ears were large and pointed and his hair hung in thin, straggly strands across his forehead and down the back of his neck. He appeared to be a man and he spoke like a man, but he looked like a werewolf with animal ears and doglike teeth. He walked like a human but he ran like an old man with a hobbled leg. I closed my eyes and prayed. My heart pounded in my ears as he aggressively started to run toward the room.

I tried to shut the door again with all my might. I was scared. The only thing I could think of was that I wanted my mother. I screamed using all my energy: "MAMA!" I yelled. My eyes went wide as I suddenly heard my voice.

The child appeared at my side and we both forcibly closed the door together. The door shut, just in time while the dog-man stood behind it, breathing heavily and making subtle accusations and threats: "You will pay for this," he growled as he sauntered away.

I stared at the child. She had a face. She had a name.

I recognized her.

She was my mother.

I awoke, drenched with sweat, my heart racing and full of panic. I jumped out of my bed and aggressively looked for her.

I called her name: "Mama? Sarah?"

I scrambled around and looked under my furniture. What does this mean? Why was my mother's image making its way into my brain? Why was her vision constantly haunting me today?

"Please, Mom! What does this mean?" I lay in bed and tried to calm myself. I took deep breaths and closed my eyes. Then it happened. The ladybug. She landed on my nose.

I took a deep sigh and laid my head on the pillow. "Okay, Mom. You win. I don't know what this means, but I'm listening. I'm waiting, patiently." I looked at my little friend as I watched her crawl all over my hand and in between my fingers. I closed my eyes and fell asleep. There were no more dreams tonight. Just peace. Just tonight.

CHAPTER 5

Sam

It had been long enough. Sam hadn't heard from Kat in six weeks.

Sam talked herself into driving by Demetry's house for the one-hundredth time and decided to pull over and get out. Why was Kat doing this to her? They've gone through so much together. If she could just talk to her, Sam thought, she could convince her, show her how important she was to her.

Sam opened her car door and shut it carefully, not wanting to draw attention to her vehicle. She walked up the steps to the front door and knocked on the screen. "Kat?" she called into the house. The main door was open and she could see into the kitchen. No one answered. Sam opened the screen and walked into the room and looked around her. The house was somewhat tidy; a few beer bottles lingered on the counter along with a stack of mail. "Kat?" she yelled again, more forcefully this time.

She walked through the hallway and into Kat's bedroom. Her room looked neat and organized and somewhat deserted. Did she move out? Sam poked around and opened a few empty dresser drawers. She found a picture of Kat and Lucy along with some other people she didn't recognize. She walked into Kat's bathroom and noticed all of her toiletries were gone. "That's weird," she murmured. Sam continued to move slowly around Kat's bedroom, touching the few remnants of her personal items, grabbing hold of a sweatshirt Kat had left behind hanging on the back of her bedroom door. Sam held the sweatshirt to her face and closed her eyes, breathing Kat's scent in deeply and then tossing the sweatshirt angrily across the bed. She sat down helplessly on the soft mattress as she began to think about the time they'd spent together in this room. She missed her deeply and vowed to do everything she could to get her back.

Sam could hear faint music coming from somewhere in the house. She walked back into the hallway and put her ear against one of the doors. It was coming from the basement.

"I've broken in this far, might as well keep going," Sam convinced herself. She opened the door and walked down the

44

stairs. She could see the haze of smoke and smell the pungent scent of skunk as she entered the stairwell of the basement.

"Hello?" she yelled over the music.

Demetry jumped up from the small table situated in the middle of the room as Sam made her way down the stairs.

"What the hell? What are you doing here? Get the hell out of my basement!" Demetry yelled.

Sam ignored him and continued to enter the main cellar. She was stunned by what she saw. She circled the room quickly, inspecting the space she had never seen before.

"Don't yell at me, Demetry! What the hell are *you* doing here?" Sam yelled back. Sam took in the fluorescent lighting and the rows of pot plants that were laid out in front of her. "So, this is what you do, Demetry? You grow and sell weed? I knew you were no good. Kat always defended you, but I knew." Sam walked around the small table, pointing her judgmental finger at Demetry.

"You need to leave before I call the police," Demetry demanded.

Sam started to laugh. "Oh, yes, please Demetry. Call the police. I'm sure they would be very interested in what you have going on here."

"What do you want, Sam? Kat's not here." Demetry sat back down and casually broke apart a bud he had pulled from a pot plant.

"Where is she? I need to speak with her."

"You haven't heard from her?" Demetry questioned sarcastically. "I wonder why that is?" He smiled at her, taunting her.

"Stop fucking with me, Demetry. I swear I'll go to the police."

Demetry stopped what he was doing and stared at Kat with disdain. He stood and grabbed her arm.

"Get out of my house. No one invited you here."

Sam started to complain as Demetry dragged her up the stairs and pushed her through the hallway to the kitchen door.

"Do what you need to do, but I'm not telling you where Kat is. She's not here, that's all you need to know."

Sam made one last attempt at forcing information out of Demetry. "Well, I guess I'll need to go to her father then. Maybe he knows where Kat is. Perhaps I need to have a conversation with him, something I should have done a long time ago."

Demetry shoved Sam through the screen door and out of the house.

"You need to forget Kat, Sam. She has moved on. There's nothing you can do about it."

Sam stood on the stoop and looked at Demetry. Who does he think he is, talking to her like this?

"Go fuck yourself, Demetry."

Demetry slammed the door in her face and locked the deadbolt.

"Son of a bitch," she said to herself as she made her way back down to her car. Sam opened the door and sat in the driver's seat. Her heart was broken, her focus worried and confused. What was happening to her Kat?

She needed to find out.

CHAPTER 6

Lucy

I rose the following morning with severe anxiety. I ran down the stairs and put on my sneakers. It was early. Maybe if I ran a few miles, I could shake this feeling out of me. It was a Saturday morning and my father was home for the day. I scribbled a quick note on the chalkboard to let him know what I was doing.

I walked out of the house and managed a few stretches before I slowly started my jog down the road. I thought about Jack. I wondered and worried about him, now that he was back in Indiana. I missed him terribly, considering the possibility that I might have made a big mistake. What if he moves on with his life? We were never given a chance; what if his feelings for me weren't as strong as I thought they were? The anxious feelings that I was experiencing, perhaps they were because of the choices I made regarding Jack. It pained me to live without him, but I had no other choice. Strange things were happening all around me and I wasn't sure how to handle it. I had no one to turn to; I had to get my life under control.

I've never been big on exercise. I suppose I've never had to worry about it. Every inch of my body was telling me to run now. I felt the anxiety everywhere—my legs, my arms, and my chest. I convinced myself that I could manage the 1½-mile run around my neighborhood roads and back. I was hoping that it was long enough to expel some energy, but I wasn't much of a runner. I hoped I didn't collapse along the way, weak and frail and beaten.

I started my jog and I tried not to think about the dream. I tried not to think about my mother. I focused on the houses I passed. I counted the number of black vehicles I saw along the way. I counted the number of bikes in people's driveways. I counted the cats and the dogs. I waved to neighbors and focused on the road ahead of me.

It was inevitable. My thoughts. The images. They found their way into my mind. I closed my eyes briefly and I listened to the birds in the trees. I listened to the pavement as my feet ran and crunched the stone and sand beneath me.

The visions. They started slowly, entering my mind like a slow-moving vehicle. It reminded me of that moment when I was young. The moment the police car drove past me with Charles in the back seat. I could feel and sense the car approaching; I felt it at my back. I saw the car, first to my right, out of the corner of my eye; I turned my head to look. I watched it move slowly past me and I followed Charles' dark and angry eyes as he stared. I watched the vehicle until it disappeared in front of me, until it was gone. The images were slow moving like the vehicle, brief and quick, but steady and purposeful.

A pool. The sounds of the children laughing and splashing ringing in my ears.

I opened my eyes and shook my head. Maybe I should take the kids swimming today. I smiled, content with the thought of swimming. Maybe my mother wanted us to have some fun. I ran past the last few houses before I entered my street. I felt a sense of calm come over my body. The running, it definitely helped.

I walked the last quarter mile to my house so I could relax my heart rate. I spoke softly to my mother: "Mama, do you want me to take the kids swimming today?" I asked and waited. I laughed to myself; what an idiot I must sound like.

"Well, I'm going to. I hope this makes you happy."

I walked into my house and grabbed bottled water out of the refrigerator. I looked outside and observed the sun rising in the sky. I felt the perspiration from my skin cling to my shirt as I watched the morning clouds make way for the sunshine. Today was going to be a good day. Today we would have some fun.

I packed lunches, towels, and sunblock into my mother's old beach bag. I called Amelia to let her know that we would be at the pool today. I could hear her scream over the phone line, her excitement overwhelming me. She worked as a lifeguard, a job my brother wasn't happy about. My brother Tommy was working at the local steel plant for the summer. He was hoping to save enough spending money to get him through the next school year. Tommy and Amelia had so many plans for each other, their lives moving forward, a life purpose in place. I was envious of them, but happy they had each other.

Amelia assured me that she would make sure the lifeguards involved my younger siblings in the organized pool games, to keep them busy. I thanked her and told her that I'd see her soon. She squealed as she hung up the phone. I loved that girl. She made me feel special.

Kaylan and Jessica were waiting for me in the kitchen, their chins on the back of their hands, resting on the counter. I laughed to myself. "You two are awfully patient!" I said.

"Can we go now?" Kaylan asked, irritated. "We can walk ourselves to the pool, Lucy. We're old enough to go alone, why do we need to wait?"

"Don't be in such a hurry, Kaylan. You can give me another five minutes. Let me round up Mikey. You can wait in the car if you like," I suggested. Kaylan and Jessica grabbed their bags and walked out of the house, arguing over who was sitting where in the car.

I rolled my eyes, climbed the stairs and opened Mikey's bedroom door. He was lying on his bed face down in his pillow.

"Come on buddy. We're waiting for you. Don't you want to swim today?" I looked at Mikey while he lay still on his bed. I observed how big he's grown, how tall he was. He's not the little baby he used to be. He was in middle school now and growing like a weed. Seeing his legs stretched out on the bed made it all the more obvious. I gently tugged on his arm. He turned his face away from me.

"What's wrong, Mikey? You don't want to come?" I asked. I could tell he's been crying and was embarrassed. I sat down on the bed next to him. "Do you miss Mama?" I asked him softly. He slowly nodded his head yes.

These moments were difficult. It was heartbreaking, to see him suffering. I remember when I was young, the fear I had of losing my mother. I was older now, I understood more, but Mikey was still young. I'm sure it was terrifying to him, his heart aching over the loss of our mother. I rubbed his back and I sat quietly and waited for him to gather himself. Mikey sat up and put his head on my shoulder. "I'm sorry, buddy. I know this is hard," I explained. "It's okay to be upset and sad. I wanted to take you swimming today so you can have a little fun. That's what Mama would want for you." I looked down at my little brother. I made a mental note to talk to Tommy. He needed to make an effort to spend more time with Mikey. He needed to keep him busy doing healthy things.

Mikey dried his eyes. "I miss her. I don't want to go to the pool without her. It doesn't feel right. She always brought us, every summer," he whimpered.

I took a deep breath. *I don't want to go to the pool without her either.*

"Why don't we say a prayer together, to Mama? Then we'll go to the pool. If it's too difficult, we'll leave. Okay, Mikey?"

53

"You say the words," Mikey said as he looked up at me.

I grabbed his hand. "Close your eyes. In the name of the Father, Son, and Holy Spirit. Dear Lord. God bless my mother today. Help her to watch over us and keep us safe. Show us a sign that she is near and that she is listening. We miss her dearly and pray for her soul. Amen."

"Amen," Mikey echoed. Mikey looked up at me as I stood to get his bathing suit.

"What does that mean, show us a sign?" Mikey asked curiously.

I glanced back at my little brother and smiled. "Well, I believe that Mama is here, with us, always watching. If you pay attention, you can look for the signs that indicate her spirit is near. Like for example, I see ladybugs in the strangest places and at the strangest times. I think that's Mama's way of saying hello, and that's she's still here for us."

Mikey's eyes opened wide. "I've seen the ladybug!" he stated excitedly. "A ladybug sat on my handlebars all day yesterday. Even when I was pedaling real fast, the ladybug didn't move. I thought it was so strange, how she hung on."

I nodded as I listened to Mikey talk. "That's what I mean, Mikey. Mama's spirit is still with us. It's just different now."

Mikey stood and walked over to his dresser to put on his bathing suit. He had a little smile on his face.

"Are you ready, Mikey?" I asked.

"Yes. I hope I see more ladybugs today."

I laughed. "I hope so too, buddy. Now lets get in the car before your sisters kill each other."

My father gave me my mother's car to transport the kids around for the summer. I was so relieved and grateful for the convenience of having it. My father didn't want us to be stuck in the house all summer doing nothing. It definitely helped to keep everyone busy.

I pulled out of the driveway carefully and started our drive toward the town pool. It was only a ten-minute ride, but it beat walking. I rolled down the windows and let the warm air hit our faces. It was going to be a hot day, I could tell. We drove down the road past the old Christmas Tree farm on the corner. I remembered the first time Jack and I kissed in the middle of those Christmas trees. A stab of pain entered my chest as I thought about Jack. I missed him terribly and thought about him obsessively. I couldn't wait to see him again, and I dreamt about it often. I turned the radio on.

Jessica yelled from the back seat, "Leave it! It's Mom's favorite song, Lucy!"

We drove in our car, singing along to the music, the breeze through our windows. I smiled as I pulled into the parking lot, Mikey still singing his weird rendition of the song. We exited the car giggling and laughing at his funniness.

"Okay, little rock star. Do you think you can grab the bags now and help out with the cooler?" I asked. He laughed and grabbed a bag.

"Mikey, maybe you should sign up for the talent show next year. You can be a comedian!" Jessica suggested sarcastically.

"Only if I can make fun of you two!" he countered, pointing at Kaylan and Jessica.

Kaylan rolled her eyes. "Oh god," she said under her breath.

"Come on, guys, let's go get some chairs before they're all gone," I said.

We walked up the short hill toward the pool area and entered the gated fence. I showed the girl working behind the desk my summer pass. I saw Amelia sitting in her chair and waved. She stood and waved frantically, like she was afraid we wouldn't notice her. I walked through the kiddie section and found three chairs together along the opposite side of the pool. Mikey threw his towel on the chair and ran off for a swim. Jessica and Kaylan sat and applied sunscreen and pulled out their *Glamour* magazines. I walked over to Amelia to say hello. I knew we couldn't talk for too long because she could get in trouble for being distracted.

"Hey Amelia! I saw you waving. You almost fell off your station," I said, laughing.

"Oh, Lucy. I'm so happy to see you out and about. I signed Mikey up for Marco Polo at 11:30. He'll like that. It fills quickly, so I put his name down," Amelia said proudly.

"Thank you. I'll tell him," I replied.

"I'm off at 3:00 today. If you're still here, I'll come sit with you."

"Okay. We'll be here for a while. We have nothing else to do."

"Great, I'll find you later," she said cheerfully.

I waved up at her as she sat back down in her lifeguard chair. I walked over to Jessica and Kaylan and settled into my lawn chair. Mikey jumped in and out of the water. I could see that a few of his friends were there. I hoped that they would play Marco Polo as well. He seemed better now. He seemed happy for the moment.

I sat back in my chair and closed my eyes. I thought about Jack again. I was hoping to get a letter today. We've been writing back and forth ever since my father received our first phone bill the month after my mother died. I thought he was going to have a heart attack. I guess it was expensive to call Indiana. So now we write. It's harder, but at least it's something.

I considered telling Jack about my anxiety. About the visions and the nightmares. I was afraid he wouldn't believe me or that he would think that I was crazy. I wished there was someone I could confide in, someone who could answer some of my questions. I took a deep breath.

I watched Kaylan and Jessica as they took a love survey out of the magazine. I focused my attention on them and asked them to include my answers in the love test. They got excited and sat closer to me. They took turns asking me the questions. I smiled at their silliness. I watched Mikey out of the corner of my eye. Today was a good day.

CHAPTER 7

Kathryn

Kat watched as the sun set beyond the oceans horizon, spilling orange and red flashes of twinkle over the water's motion. They just pulled into port after a smooth day of fishing off Boston's harbor. One tuna. One very large tuna. Charles was so happy and proud.

Kat's never seen fishing like this before. While she watched Charles and Jimmy fight and struggle with the massive fish, pulling it in from the rugged ocean waters, she nervously lingered in the cabin, trying to be helpful. Charles had given her several lessons on driving the twenty-foot, beat-up, barely-making-it fishing boat. She was pretty good at it. There wasn't much to it, actually. The hard part was when Charles caught a fish, it was a little tricky keeping the boat steady but Charles said that she was doing a good job. She was in charge of cleaning the deck and carefully she cut the bait every morning and tossed the nasty fish into the ocean to lure the tuna. She felt lucky to be a part of the crew. She was really impressed with Charles; his knowledge was expansive. Years of working on fishing boats had prepared him for running his own boat, his hard work paying off.

She and Charles had rented a small two-bedroom apartment and they leased the boat and dock from a friend of a man Charles used to work for. The man was really helpful, encouraging Charles to get on his feet. So far, it was a very successful endeavor. Charles convinced their neighborhood friend, Jimmy Daniels, to help him on the boat for the summer. Jimmy was down and out and jumped at the opportunity. It was a little awkward at first, the three of them living together, but she was used to living with Demetry. She adjusted well when it came to men. It was hard for Charles and her to get any privacy with Jimmy around, but fortunately Jimmy spent a lot of his time at the local tavern, aware of their tight quarters. Sometimes, he would even stay on the boat, if the weather were right.

She thought about her family. She felt pangs of guilt when she thought about Lucy and her father. Her father was supportive regarding her decision to try commercial fishing. She wasn't sure whether he really cared, other than she was one less person to worry about. She sent them postcards and pictures of the fish they caught. She called Lucy weekly to see how everyone was coping. Lucy seemed busy and preoccupied but always cheerful when they spoke. Kat promised her she'd be home by the end of the summer, but Charles talked about buying his own boat and heading down south. If they made enough money, that is. The thought of traveling down south and seeing different things was exciting for her. For the first time in her life she felt encouraged. She felt like she had a purpose, and perhaps a life with Charles. Every day, she felt more for him. She thought she even loved him. She wasn't sure where life would lead them, Charles and her, but she was eager to find out. She was staying the course and she looked forward to the experiences that lay ahead of them.

"Hey, Kat. Can you give me a hand?" Kat shook herself out of her thoughtful stare and turned around to see Jimmy staring at her. "You look very intense. Are you okay?" he asked.

She stood from her bench and turned to walk toward the deck of the boat. "Sorry, I was just enjoying the sunset." She scooted past Jimmy, sensing his eyes boring into her suntanned skin, and turned back quickly to give him a nasty look.

"What?" he asked, smiling.

She rolled her eyes and helped him with the anchor.

CHAPTER 8

Sam

Sam drove herself home from Demetry's on autopilot. She had no awareness of where she was going or how she was driving. When she arrived in her driveway, she was thankful her mind subconsciously knew how to get her home. Her eyes were swollen and red. Frustration was racking her body as she leaned over her steering wheel, trying to gather and calm herself. She began to hit her head against it, unaware of how hard and how violent she shook. She felt so alone without Kat; how could she manage without her? And Demetry, he was laughing at her for sure.

Sam sat in her car oblivious to all the vehicles in her mother's driveway. She had forgotten her mother was hosting a luncheon for the ladies at the club, an event Sam was supposed to co-host and help her with. There was no way she could do that now. Sam knew her mother would be angry. Sam was expected to be the perfect daughter, pretty and presentable at all times. She was expected to be a good student, straight A's and well spoken. Sam knew if she walked into that house now, her mother would look at her quietly, disapproving of her lateness and lack of proper luncheon attire.

Growing up, Sam and her family were fortunate to have wealth and prosperity, her father a well-known lawyer in town, her mother an established artist. These luncheons were common and fused over, most of her mother's friends avid fans of her paintings and falling over themselves to be in her presence. Sam knew that her mother loved the attention. Her mother aspired to have a perfect family, outwardly. Inwardly, Sam knew that her parents were whispering and judging her, saying things like, "We expected more from you, Sam." Many nights she spent alone in her room, dealing with her parents' silent treatments over the slightest infractions, such as missing the luncheon or perhaps forgetting to make her bed in the morning. Sam was never good enough. There was always something she did wrong to dissatisfy them.

The constant disappointment and Sam's inability to meet her parents' expectations crushed her. Sam realized now that she behaved the same way toward Kat. Sam was constantly bashing her, judging her, silently disapproving. Sam was desperate to get another chance. Without Kat, she was a failure. Her life would never be the same; she needed Kat to love her again. Kat was the only one who ever did.

How was she going to get into her house without her mother intercepting her? Sam couldn't deal with her mother now. She needed to keep an eye on Demetry. She would watch him and follow him. Sam knew that eventually he would lead her to Kat. Demetry had to know where Kat was, he was Sam's only hope to get to her.

Sam started her car once again and backed slowly out of her driveway. Her parents wouldn't be proud of her, she knew, but her life wasn't perfect anymore. She couldn't find any happiness without Kat. Kat stabilized her and kept her balanced. Without her, she might as well be dead.

CHAPTER 9

Jack

I received a call from Lucy today, which was rare. I could tell that she had her hands full and I wished that I could help her. She said that she needed to hear my voice, that she was having a hard day.

She was still so confused over her mother's passing. The mental breakdown and illness took hold of her mother so fast, leaving her family to question the reasons why. I told her that her feelings of loss and sadness would eventually subside over time. I tried to offer words of comfort and told her that what she was feeling was normal. She tried to convince me that she was okay and that she was handling it just fine. I could tell that she didn't want to burden me. Her strength and focus amazed me. She was born a natural mother and nurturer. I needed her; I missed her warm smile and easy ways. I clung to the memories and thought of her constantly. I could visualize her pretty face, her eyes confident yet vulnerable.

I begged her to come visit. I offered to drive and pick her up for a few days; I promised it would be short and simple and that she'd be back home with her family in no time. She hesitated. I knew the answer would be no, but she hesitated. I thought about her, and then I thought about Angie. Angie was not giving up on me, or on our relationship. She was constantly around me. Lucy and Angie were so different. They were both wonderful in their own ways but worlds apart. Angie was a farmer; she understood the life that I lived. She understood the farm and she was not afraid to put her hands into the dirt. I loved that about her. She knew far more about farming than I could only hope to know and understand. She worked hard and I respected her. Angie wanted to understand my life, where I came from. She wanted to know everything she could about me. She wanted me to confide in her and it was hard to resist her. Angie showed real concern and attention and it felt nice to have someone show affection.

I wished Lucy were here. I needed her here. I couldn't live like this forever. I understood that she needed to take care of her family now but it was difficult to accept. If only we lived in the same state, it would be easier. I felt so confused. I felt so angry. I lost everything when I was young. I lost my home, my mother, my friends, Lucy. But then Pop found me, and then Lucy and Charles found me. Now, they are gone again. I almost wish they left me be. I was starting my life over. Angie and I were having fun. I was happy. Now my heart was broken all over again. This wasn't fair. I wanted to feel normal.

CHAPTER 10

Demetry

Demetry entered his mother's house, drained from the argument they had during their earlier conversation. His mother was worried about him, he understood. But her constant nagging and harassment was not helping him. Her phone calls were annoying and exhausting. He wanted to be left alone. He didn't want her advice or interference or suggestions. He could handle his problems on his own.

Demetry's mother had always wanted him to join her in the family business, a successful organization that had been passed down to her by her father. Demetry loved to help her and was supportive of her when she needed him. His mother ran a kennel, but not just any kind of kennel. She trained German Shepherds for the blind and had a particular niche for training special unit police dogs, trained to hunt, track, attack, and kill if need be. Demetry had grown up with these animals and was highly skilled at training them and caring for them. Unfortunately, to his mother's dismay, Demetry disliked police officers. For obvious reasons, he preferred to keep his distance from them.

Demetry sat at his mother's table and waited for her to walk into the kitchen. He looked at the pile of prescription medicines lying on the counter with his name on them, then outside the kitchen sink window where he saw his mother working with Molly, one of his favorite dogs. He grabbed the prescriptions and threw them carelessly into this backpack and walked behind the house to join his mother.

"Hey Mom," he said without looking at her face. He knelt down next to Molly and hugged her roughly, playing with her eagerly as he rolled around the grass with her. It felt good, to be with Molly. She understood him.

"Did you get the pills?" his mother asked.

"Yup."

"Have you talked to Kat?"

"Nope."

"I'm worried about you. I don't want you to fall into that place again. It's not healthy. You need to stay on top of your medication, do you understand?"

Demetry looked into Molly's face and mimicked his mother as he spoke.

"*Do you understand?*" he said in a whining, irritated mockery of his mother. He turned back and glared at his mother. "Don't mention Kat to me again. Do *you* understand?"

CHAPTER 11

Lucy

Every night, roughly around dinnertime, my sister Kaylan had gotten into the bad habit of begging to sleep with me. It would start at the supper table, her relentless harassment ringing in my ear: "Please, Lucy.... Just this one time?"

Kaylan was sweet and helpful at times, but also difficult and very stubborn. When she got an idea in her head, she refused to let it go. If I didn't agree with her ideas, she would harass me until I did. She was scared to be alone at night, and I understood her feelings. I wouldn't mind if she slept with me, other than I was afraid that it would detour my mother from her visit. I decided to take the risk tonight. Kaylan obviously needed to feel some sort of comfort and reassurance from me. I wanted to give her that, if I could. I was pretty sure that she was having restless nights like the rest of us.

Kay jumped into my bed and snuggled up with my good pillow. I laughed at her. "You're not taking my pillow," I said sternly. She threw the pillow back at me.

"You big baby," she said, giggling. Kaylan pulled the sheets away from the mattress and crawled underneath them. I watched her as she settled in, remembering when we were kids sharing a bedroom and a bed. My room back then was different, full of mismatched furniture and random pictures hanging on the walls. Now my room was cozy and comfortable. A warm glow radiated from my bedside lamp, casting shadows and illuminating light onto my soft blue walls and cream-colored curtains. Kathryn's collection of old vinyl records still sat in a pile on top of a linen cabinet littered on one side with used school books and tattered, heavily read beach novels. My mother's bed quilts were stacked high on the other side of the cabinet; framed pictures of our various childhood artwork hung on my walls.

"Go to sleep, Kaylan. This is your one and only chance," I warned. "We're definitely getting too old for this, don't you think?" I teased as I tickled her.

"I know, I just can't sleep at night. I hate bedtime."

74

I knew how she felt. We lay close to each other. I shut my light off.

"Do you remember when Mom would tuck us in at night and tell us the bedtime story she wrote when we were little? You know, the one where she changes the name of the little princess to our names? The one with the colors and the vegetable garden?" Kaylan asked quietly.

I thought about her question and I could hear my mother's voice echoing in my memory. "I remember, Kaylan. I remember how she used to change her voice and talk like a little princess. She made funny faces and hand gestures to animate the story. Hey! We should write that story down, so we don't forget it. That would be a good project we can work on," I suggested.

Kaylan's eyes lit up in the darkness as she smiled. "That's an awesome idea. We can draw pictures and make it into a real book, for Mom."

"I think that's a great idea, Kaylan. Try to go to sleep now. You need the rest."

Kaylan turned on her side and began to settle in.

"Lucy?" she asked.

"Yeah?"

"Thank you," she whispered softly.

I put my hand on her head and played with her hair. "Goodnight, Kay."

"Night."

I waited until I heard Kaylan's heavy breathing, a clear sign that she had fallen asleep. I prayed to my mother to watch over us and to protect us always.

I thought about our busy afternoon. I thought about all the anxiety I had endured, ever since my mother died. Was it normal, to feel so much anxiety? Perhaps it was a part of the mourning process, the worry and stress of trying to do the right things. Not really knowing what all the right things were. When I woke this morning, I thought the day ahead of me was going to be awful. Coping with the anxiety had been a constant in my life, an awareness that I tried to keep controlled. I tried to convince myself that the anxiety was all in my head, that it was fear trying to take over. I said over and over again, "Don't be afraid. Don't be afraid."

I was afraid. I feared that if I let the anxiety take over, I wouldn't be able to stop myself from falling apart. I feared that I would collapse from it, hyperventilate and explode from within the inside. I tried not to ignore it; I tried to keep my brain focused and occupied on positive things. I needed to block the random thoughts and visions that entered my mind daily, creating the anxiety and adding to the chaos. When I was aware of my brain's random activity and present in the moment, I was able to control my thinking and decrease the anxiety. I was starting to recognize the anxious feelings as they entered my chest and flooded my body. I ran, I exercised; I did everything I could to keep it at bay.

Jack popped into my mind. I thought about our time together. I fixated on it, analyzed it, and relived it. My heart ached for him. I would dream of his touch and think about his love, fantasize about the time we spent. He needed me; I could tell; something felt wrong. It was hard to explain but I knew he wasn't happy. I wish I could go to him, but I couldn't. My father would never allow it now. My father was not interested in entertaining my young love affair when he had just lost the love of his life. He wasn't interested in anything at this point. He was angry and he was depressed. If I could fast forward the clock and rush our family's mourning into high speed, I would. I would skip this depressing, dark period in our lives. I would move forward and live in a world where life was happening and where people were happy and joyful.

I laid my head back on my pillow and tried desperately to relax. I closed my eyes and felt the heaviness overcome them. My mind went blank, my body heavy with weight and sleepiness.

The dream began. I was hiding in a basement. I could tell it was a basement from the musty odor of earth and mold. I moved my foot carefully on the ground and I could feel that the basement floor beneath me was compact with dirt and small pieces of stone. I crouched down against the door, willing my eyes to focus on the darkness, waiting for them to adjust to the lighting and hopeful that I may see what lay ahead of me, in that basement. My heart was pounding and I recognized that terrifying feeling. I looked around for young Sarah. She was here with me, somewhere. I could sense her fear and struggle. I felt that she spent a lot of time in this basement, locked away and hidden from the others.

I stood slowly, pressing my body against the door that supported me from behind. I took several steps forward, but I remained walking in place, getting nowhere. The basement appeared to be growing larger and larger and there was nowhere to hide. I could feel the cool, metal door at my back, but it was dark still and my eyes were clouded. I tried to turn the doorknob, but it was locked and unmoving.

A small light hung from the ceiling, moving back in forth as if someone had pushed it, but no one was there. I was desperate to see daylight, but there were no windows.

The door handle behind me turned. Someone was twisting the knob, slowly, intentionally, trying to be discreet. I quickly stood away from the door and turned to look at it. I watched the rusted, rounded knob continue to move, back and forth, resisting the individual on the other side. Whoever was there became instantly impatient as he began banging on the door, startling me into reaction, my legs starting to work and move again. My chest exploding out of my body, my hands shaking as panic began to settle in around my heart.

It was the man; he was after us again. I turned to run and reached for the stairwell. The stairs were my only hope to escape the basement. The man was aggressively pulling on the door; the hinges were rattling, his voice strangely empty and desperate as he screamed Sarah's name.

He was swearing and calling at her: "You little bitch. Answer me! You little whore! Open this door!"

I ran, my heart breaking from his hurtful words as I desperately tried to reach the stairs. I looked around me at all the corners of the darkened room. I looked for her, hoping she was

79

hiding where I could not see her, hoping she was safe from the man behind the door.

"Sarah!" I screamed. "Where are you? Run Sarah, run!"

I reached the stairs and climbed the broken down, battered steps. I looked ahead at the top of the stairwell. The door was glowing with bright light—freedom.

The steps were endless. They continued like I was walking on the escalator at the mall. I ran for my life. I ran for Sarah.

The steps continued. I was never going to reach the door.

The man, he was coming for us. He was able to rip open the door and he angrily lunged through the basement space, looking for us.

"Sarah!" I yelled. "Please, help me!"

I turned back nervously to look at the man who was chasing me. His face was lined with wrinkles and wiry looking facial hair randomly scattered along his cheeks and jawbone. I could smell his breath; a nasty scent of rotten flesh emanated from his being. He glared at me. His eyes were golden in color but appeared to be hollow inside. I could see my reflection in them as they narrowed in on me.

He started to run toward me, his appearance frightful, stunning me into stillness, shocked as I looked at him, not sure of what to make of his bizarre figure.

I stumbled as I panicked, my hands and arms reaching out to stop my fall against the wooden stairs. Dirt and dust scattered across my face and clothing and into my mouth as I fell.

I scrambled desperately to stand on my feet, the man quickly hovering over me as my body shook, the sounds of fear and terror bursting out of my mouth as I cried, "MOM!"

She appeared.

Sarah. She floated through me, up the stairs, toward the doorway. I felt her spirit pass through my chest and watched her image lead me to safety. Her soul's sudden invasion was shocking yet exhilarating and peaceful.

My gasping chest calmed briefly in the moment, lost to my confused senses as I experienced something supernatural.

Distracted only briefly, the scary wolf-man began howling his words of hatred and threats of unforgivable pain and torture while grabbing at my feet. His voice growling as he spoke,

81

spit and phlegm dripping from his jaw as his lips curled around his jagged teeth.

I jumped and moved my feet quickly, avoiding his aggressive efforts. I felt anger toward him, and a sudden surge of confidence enveloped me as I kicked him in his face and watched him as he fell down the basement stairs. He glared up at me as I turned to look at him one last time. There was something familiar about his face. I sensed evil. Pure evil.

We passed through the glowing door and slammed it shut behind us. My heart thrummed against my chest as I threw myself against the closed door. I felt my back scrape against the wood grain as we slumped down to the ground. I looked over at Sarah and she looked over at me. My eyes were wide with fear and my upper body, blasting out of my ribcage. Sarah's eyes were dark and doll-like, but then she smiled. She smiled at me.

I was awake.

Kaylan was shaking me. "Lucy! Lucy! Wake up!"

I opened my eyes and I saw Kaylan staring down at me, trying to wake me.

"I'm awake, Kaylan, I'm awake."

"Are you okay? You were screaming in your sleep."

I sat up and reached for the glass of water I left on my bed stand. I took a sip and gathered myself.

Kaylan grabbed a cloth and wiped the sweat off my forehead.

"I'm sorry, Kaylan. I must have had a nightmare."

"It sounds it," she said with concern. "You scared me half to death."

"I'm alright, you can go back to bed now," I said unconvincingly.

"Geez, Lucy," she said as she turned over and went back to sleep. She glanced back at me to make certain that I was all right and I nodded to reassure her.

I saw out of the corner of my eye a shadow. I watched as it moved across the room and into the hallway. Every hair on my body was standing at attention. Goosebumps moved up and down the back of my neck and arms. The shadow was gone in a split second, but I saw it. I knew what it was. I lay back on my pillow. I pulled the sheets tight around my neck. My heart strained against the insides of my body. I moved my leg to touch Kay's for comfort. I was so glad Kaylan was there, in my bed. I was so glad she insisted on sleeping with me. Kaylan reached over and held my hand tight. There would be no more dreaming tonight. There would be no more sleeping. Who needed sleep anyway?

Apparently, not me.

CHAPTER 12

Lucy

I promised Amelia I would pick her up after work today. I drove quietly through town and pulled up into the winding parking lot toward the pool. Thoughts of Jack continued to dominate my quiet time.

I was tired of crying. I cried for my mother, I cried for Jack, alone in my bed at night. My heart was broken all around; my only joy would be to see him again, to be with him, to see his eyes and feel safe in his arms. I needed him. I missed him desperately.

I kept an internal calendar in my head, trying to figure out when would be a good time to leave my family. When was it ever going to be a good time? If I leave next year, Kaylan would be the next responsible one. Maybe my father would be okay then. Maybe he would come around from the pain and could find joy once again within his children. My father was my only hope. He needed to be okay for us. My life eventually needed to move on.

I was thinking of Jack and listening to the music in the car, oblivious to the commotion that surrounded me, when suddenly an ambulance and fire truck overtook me. The abrupt sirens and lights surprised and startled me and I took a minute to relax my shaking hands. I quickly pulled over and parked my car.

Something bad was happening. The image, kids jumping and swimming in the pool, popped into my head again. I started to run up the short hill toward the pool area and before I could enter it, a staff member stopped me.

"Is everything okay?" I asked.

"Please, stay where you are. A child's been injured and they're trying to get her help."

I looked past the young man and immediately, I felt my lungs fill with water. I tried to cough and catch my breath but my chest was tight and constricted. I ran over to the fence and vomited in the grass.

"Are you alright?" the man asked, slightly disgusted.

"Yes, I'll be fine," I replied, my stomach turning as I thought about the small child.

I looked through the fence for Amelia. Relief flooded my body as I saw her running on the concrete patio carrying towels and a pillow. I couldn't see the child, but I could sense the situation was desperate. Other parents and lifeguards were rushing around, trying to be helpful. Children were being ushered away from the situation and I could hear a woman crying and screaming.

"Help her! Help her, dear god, please! Help her!"

I said a quick, quiet prayer for the help and safety of the child. The EMTs ran through the pool area, placing the little girl on a gurney and quickly rushing her to the ambulance. I watched as the mother jumped into the back of the ambulance with her daughter. The ambulance rushed away with its sirens screaming, leaving the rest of us in shock and dismay. Fire trucks and other emergency vehicles slowly followed suit as the dramatic scene started to calm down.

A woman appeared at my side. I looked up at her. I didn't know this woman but I could sense that she wanted to talk to me. She stared ahead at the pool and began to speak.

"Your feelings are special. Not everyone can sense things, see things, but I know that you can."

I opened my mouth to respond but then I closed it again. I had no idea what to say. I knew the child had died. I felt her slip away as my heart stopped beating for a few seconds; my chest tightened suddenly, desperate for air. I could hear the mother screaming in my ear, a high-pitched wail that no one else could hear. I looked up at the woman and she gave me a card. In an instant, she was gone. I quickly looked for her around the pool, but she had disappeared.

I glanced at the card again. The card had three words on it: *Anna Jones, Medium.* On the back of the card was a phone number. I quickly slipped it into my pocket and went to Amelia.

Amelia was trying to catch her breath while she spoke, hysterical, distraught and upset over the drowning. Apparently, it was Amelia who had pulled the child out of the water. I rubbed her back and helped her into my car as she cried and verbally recreated the series of events for me. Out of the corner of my eye I saw the woman, Anna, standing tall on the hill, staring at me as I got into my vehicle. I stared back for a few seconds, taking in the woman's appearance and her confidence. She wore a soft, flowing white bathing suit cover and a beautiful beach hat. She looked elegant and beautiful as she stood, the wind slightly blowing the dress away from her legs.

I slowly pulled my car out of the parking lot, Amelia's well-being most important to me, but the woman... still on my mind.

CHAPTER 13

Kathryn

Kathryn walked home from the grocery store, overwhelmed by the amount of groceries that she carried. She was an over buyer, especially when she was hungry. Her apartment was only a block away, she quietly told herself; walk faster, walk faster.

She thought about the past week. Charles and Jimmy were doing well on the boat. Charles' insisted that he didn't need her on the boat every day, that they were managing fine without her. She got the sense Charles didn't want her around Jimmy.

"Jimmy's harmless," she told him. She was aware that sometimes his eyes lingered a little longer than they should. When he drank, he became a little bolder with his hugs and kisses. "He just needs a girlfriend," she said to Charles.

Charles shook his head. "I don't really care what he needs. What he'll get is a punch in his face and a quick bus ticket back home. We don't need him that bad. You and I could run this boat alone."

Kat would love being alone with Charles, but she rolled her eyes. She didn't quite understand jealousy. Sam was a jealous person as well and it always made her feel uncomfortable. Kat always thought that it was flattering when someone thought you were attractive. Why did that have to be a bad thing?

The summer was quickly coming to an end. She needed to make a decision on whether she would be returning home. She didn't want to go home, but she promised Lucy that she would help her. Kat knew in her heart that she had made her decision; she just needed to bring herself to tell Lucy. She felt happy for the first time in her life; she didn't want to disappoint Charles and she didn't want to disappoint her family. It was a difficult decision for her to make, but she was staying with Charles.

It was a warm summer evening and many people were out sitting on the stoops of their apartment buildings. When they arrived in Boston, Kat remembered driving on the interstate, watching the city appear in the near distance, the tall buildings and lights filling the skyline as the excitement of her new adventure filled her heart. She remembered going to Fenway Park

91

and walking Yawkey Way full of restaurants and bars. She and Charles explored the city together, going to Quincy Market, visiting Boston's Harbor, and driving through Harvard University.

They were poor when they arrived in Boston. Lower class people mostly populated the neighborhood where they lived. The streets were rampant with drugs and crime. She remembered how horrified she felt when she saw her first homeless man. She was walking over a bridge down a busy street lined with people and activity when she noticed the makeshift cardboard home set deep into the woods beneath her. She stopped on top of the bridge and looked down into the small patch of wilderness. A small tent and an old shopping cart full of belongings were nestled against a tree. Tarps were scattered around the ground and small lanterns hung from the branches up above. She looked over the temporary homeless shelter and felt a great deal of sadness and wonder about the person who lived there. She continued to walk on slowly, concern registering on her face as she began to accept the situation.

She loved Boston but she would be happy to settle in a different town. Charles promised her that North Carolina would be different. He talked about the beautiful seaports and the small quaint beach towns of the Outer Banks coast. The endless dunes and lighthouses, the white sand was all she longed for. She couldn't wait. He made it sound so lovely.

Kat stopped and put the grocery bags down on the ground. There was no way she could make it if she didn't take a rest.

"Hey, hey, hey baby? Whatcha got there?"

Kat looked up ahead at the man who was quickly approaching her. His face was determined and full of purpose. He moved toward her, his gold teeth gleaming, his left eye slightly slanted and scarred, his clothes hanging off his body.

"Oh god," she whispered to herself. She quickly picked up her bags and continued walking toward the opposite portion of the sidewalk.

The man continued to follow her. "Whatcha hurry honey? Don't run, I just want to talk to you. You're looking *good*, sweetheart. Baby *needs* a man."

She walked as quickly as she could. Her arms were aching from the groceries and she considered dropping them and running. She looked around for a police officer, but she knew that she probably wouldn't find one. She thought about the mace Charles had given her sitting on her kitchen counter.

"Wow, baby, you are *fine*! Why don't you give me your bags and I'll carry them for you?" the man yelled.

She started to gather her courage and began to turn around to verbally assault the man when someone pushed past her from out of nowhere and grabbed the jerk by his throat.

"What is it exactly that you need from this girl? I believe it's obvious she doesn't want you following her," Demetry yelled as he choked the man.

"I'm sorry! I'm sorry, brother! I didn't mean no harm." The man grabbed at his throat as Demetry squeezed even harder.

"Get the hell out of here!" Demetry spat as he pushed the man down on the pavement.

The man stood up and straightened himself out. He yelled back at Demetry as he walked away from them, "You're an asshole!"

Kat stood there with her groceries, stunned by Demetry's magical appearance.

"What the hell are *you* doing here?" She dropped her groceries and hugged her friend.

"I had to see you," Demetry said as he embraced her.

"Well, lucky me! Your timing couldn't be any more perfect," she said gratefully. "My apartment is right around the corner. Let's go. It can get real dangerous around here once the sun sets." She laughed.

"At least let me help you with your bags. You look ridiculous walking down the street like this." Demetry took her bags and carried them with ease.

"I know…we don't have a car."

Demetry started to laugh. "Nothing's changed, has it?"

"Shut up!" she said, grinning widely. She realized at that moment how homesick she was. Demetry's surprise visit was just what she needed. She was so happy he was here!

CHAPTER 14

Jack

I sat at my kitchen table, staring out of the window, watching the animals as they wandered around the barnyard. Susie Mae put a plate of food in front of me; the signs of worry circling her eyes as she stared at me. I picked up my fork and pushed the food around my plate. How would I make it without her, without Lucy? As I often did, I thought about how I was going to fill my night, fill the void of loneliness. I felt the frustration fill my chest as I began to eat. I took deep breaths in between the small bites of food that I could manage. I pushed the plate away from me.

"Jack, what's wrong, son?" Pop asked as he stood in the doorway, watching me.

"Nothing."

"Are you going out tonight? Perhaps there are some friends you would like to see. Maybe you could get out of the house for a little while."

"I have work to do. I need to cut that pile of wood and stack it, Pop. I don't feel much like socializing."

"I received another letter today from the University of Florida. They're still interested in meeting with you, Jack. They still want you to play football!"

I looked at my grandfather. Doesn't he understand what's happening here? I was sacrificing my time and energy, my life to be with him. Why does he keep pressuring me to go to college? I wanted to stay on the farm. It was the right thing to do.

"I don't understand, Pop. Don't you want me here? Why are you trying to push me away?"

I stood from my chair and placed my plate of food forcibly into the kitchen sink. I could feel the anger building up in my chest as the heat of my skin began to burn my neck and cheeks. I tried to remain calm and respectful while I spoke to my grandparents.

"Of course we want you here, baby." Susie Mae spoke softly. "It's just that...you seem so unhappy. We only want what's best for you."

"If I was going to leave the farm, I would go to Connecticut. That's what's best for me. That's where I should be right now, but I'm here instead, because I love you and it's important to me. Don't you get it?" I turned my back on my grandparents and walked through the screen door, toward the barn.

"Jack!" Pop yelled from the kitchen.

I ignored his calls. I needed to be alone.

I walked past the barn toward the back of the woodshed. I felt instantly guilty for being so short with Pop and Susie Mae. I knew they meant well. I know I've been in a rotten mood for weeks now; I can't seem to shake it. My feelings are tortured between Lucy and Angie. My heart is with Lucy and I love her deeply. I can't seem to settle into my decision to wait for her. I want our life to begin now. Waiting is too difficult.

I picked up the ax stuck firmly into the tree stump and swung it hard over my head. I slammed it down into the block of lumber, splitting it in two. I watched the firewood drop to the ground. Every time I swung the ax over my head, I thought about how angry I was over my situation. How unfair life has been toward me, how frustrating it was to be so far from the person I cared about the most.

I stopped for a moment to take off my shirt. Sweat had begun to pour off me. I closed my eyes and thought about Lucy. There was nothing I could do; the situation was out of my hands. She was adamant in her choice to stay in Connecticut, her decision clearly voiced to me on several occasions. I took another deep breath and continued to work, splitting the cord of wood and stacking it carefully. I couldn't help but feel rotten.

I felt her eyes on me as I worked. I ignored her. She made my life difficult; she confused me and I was angry and vulnerable. I knew she would linger for a moment before offering me the refreshing glass of water that I needed and would appreciate. I waited.

"Hey Jack," she said sweetly.

"Hi Ang..."

"Are you thirsty?"

I was. I stopped working and looked up at her pretty face. She smiled softly at me, her brown eyes innocent and genuine. I could tell her feelings for me were deep. She didn't say so, but the way she looked at me, I could tell. I watched her as she moved closer to me, her eyes locked on to mine. Her face looked determined, confident. I had never seen her look so sure.

"Thank you, Angie."

She moved in front of me while she put her hand gently on my face. I tried to turn to look away briefly but her body was so close to mine. I could see her chest move as she breathed heavily, her eyes searching mine.

"Jack, you seem so…lost," she said quietly.

I stared at her, desperately wanting to kiss her so I could feel something different. I wanted to feel something more than depression and loneliness. I wanted to feel warmth and affection. I wanted to feel love.

She placed her hands on my bare arms; she held them with conviction and pressed her chest against my naked skin. I could feel the softness of her breasts beneath her shirt. I could smell her skin and feel her breath against my face. It was too much, too much for me to resist.

I wanted her. I kissed her.

CHAPTER 15

Lucy

Dear Lucy,

It hurts me deeply to write these words that my heart hardly feels, but that I know I must say for the greater benefit to both of us. I love you, Lucy. I know you feel this. Please, don't ever forget how grateful I am to you. Your love and support has always brought comfort to me. Even in the depths of such confusion and separation, you were always there for me, unknowingly. Our time together was so special and meaningful. I've dreamt of it, time and time again. I wish you were here. I wish I could hold you again and love you, like you deserve.

My thoughts and feelings won't match the words that I need to say, the words that will hurt so deeply. I must move on. I must go forward with my life as if you never existed. To stay in this place of want and mourning is devastating me. My heart can't possibly take any more abandonment, rejection, or distance from the one that I need and love the most. It's impossible for me to live this way.

I hope you understand. I will love you always. I'm sorry.

Jack

I read the words carefully on the letter sent from Indiana. I read them again, my heart wrenching out of my chest. I read them one last time. I crumbled the letter and threw it across the room and watched it bounce against the wall. I sat on the edge of my bed, my heart rate pulsing with anger and frustration. My eyes burned from the tears that I was unwilling to shed. I shook my head back and forth in disbelief. My heart broken, I picked myself up and pulled out the business card from Anna. I needed help. I would never survive this.

I ran down the stairs with fury in my heart. My father. This was entirely his fault. Why was I stuck here doing the jobs he should be doing? Why was I sacrificing my life for the benefit of his? I wanted to be with Jack. That's where I belonged. I quickly searched the house for my father.

"Jessica, have you seen Dad?" I asked eagerly.

"Garage," she responded.

Figures. I walked out of the house, anger in my heart, tears in my eyes. I opened the garage door to confront my father. I was aware that the words I was going to say would hurt, but I didn't care. I was hurting now. I was suffering.

"Dad!" I yelled over the sanding machine.

My father looked up at me, confused. He shut off the power tool.

"What is it?" he asked, irritated that I was interrupting him.

I looked at my father. I looked at his miserable face. The bags under his eyes, the unkempt hair, the disheveled clothing he continued to wear everyday. I remember the awful words my mother would say to him. I remember how hurt my father would look when she spat such hatred at him.

"What is it, Lucy?"

I can't do it. I can't hurt him. "I was wondering what you wanted me to make for dinner?"

"Oh, whatever you feel, honey. I don't care."

"Okay, Dad. I'll fix something easy," I responded sadly.

I turned to leave the garage, my heart as broken as the day my mother died. I turned quickly so my father wouldn't see the tears flowing from my face. I had to cry. I couldn't take it. I'll never make it. I sat on the stoop and cried, and it felt good.

CHAPTER 16

Lucy

I woke the next morning feeling the devastation and loss rip through my heart all over again as I thought of Jack's message. I uncrumbled Jack's letter, folded it neatly, and placed it in my underwear drawer. I slowly got dressed and dragged myself down the stairs and made coffee.

I thought about contacting Jack, begging him to reconsider. I wanted to beg him for time; I wanted him to wait for me. As much as his words were hurtful, I knew they rang true for our circumstances. It was an unbearable situation. There was nothing we could do. We would never be together. The faster I learned to accept this, the quicker it would be for me to move on.

I sat at the kitchen counter and listened to the news on the portable television. Thomas walked down the stairs with a large duffel bag slung over his shoulder, stuffed with all his belongings.

"Wow, are you going somewhere?" I asked curiously.

"Boston," he said curtly.

"Already?"

"For the weekend. The school won't let us move in officially for another two weeks, but they have a special orientation this weekend. We're allowed to bring a few things now, to make the move easier on everyone."

I nodded my head as he spoke.

"Why are you so irritated?" I asked.

"Amelia doesn't want me to go. She's still pretty shaken up over the accident at the pool. She's a nervous wreck."

"I'll keep her occupied. I'll spend some time with her, until you get back. She'll have to start getting used to the idea of you being away at school anyway. You can't drive back and forth from Boston every day to be with her."

"I know. It's just hard. Long distance relationships don't always work out."

106

Tell me about it.

"It's only one year. Next year Amelia plans on attending Boston College just the same," I said.

"I know. We just have to make it one year." Tommy grabbed his oversized duffel bag and headed for the door.

"Have a nice weekend," I said as I casually waved him goodbye.

"See ya!" Thomas shut the door.

I waited for my brother to start his car and leave the driveway before I called Amelia. I picked up the phone and dialed her number. She answered the phone immediately.

"Hey Amelia."

"Hey," she said sadly.

"Are you okay?"

"No," she responded in a whimper.

I took a deep breath. It was hard to imagine a time when things weren't so screwed up. I wondered when that was and what that was like.

"Do you want to come over?" I asked. "I need to go see this lady. I would love it if you would come with me. Maybe she could help you too," I suggested. "She's a medium."

"A medium? What do we need a medium for?"

I thought about my dreams. I decided to tell Amelia about my visions, about my anxiety and about Jack. Perhaps it would distract her from her own problems. "I'll explain when you get here."

"Alright. I'll see you soon."

I hung up the phone.

I immediately picked up the phone again. I dialed the number that I had etched into my memory. My heart was screaming as the phone rang.

He picked up. I heard his voice. I said nothing. I stopped and listened.

"Hello? Is anyone there?" he asked.

I closed my eyes and envisioned Jack standing in his kitchen, holding the phone receiver and staring out into the yard through a window. I pictured him as he leaned his head on the side of the doorway.

I said nothing. My breathing was heavy, my chest visibly rising and falling.

"I'm sorry," he said quietly. "I'm so sorry."

I hung up.

CHAPTER 17

Kat

Demetry and Kat walked up the front stoop of the small brick building and Kat quickly shut her apartment door behind them.

Demetry placed the bags of groceries on the counter, scanning the area around him. "This is where you stay?" Demetry asked as he walked around the small apartment.

"I know it looks bad, Demetry, but it's all we can afford in the city. Boston is very expensive," she explained.

"Where's your boyfriend?" he asked as he picked up a magazine lying on the table. Some sort of live insect scattered across the space from underneath it and he quickly tossed it back on the surface, startled by the sudden movement.

"They won't be home 'til morning. They need to fish through the night to meet their quota."

"And he just leaves you here…by yourself, in this place where you get harassed walking down the street?" Demetry took a seat at the kitchen table and crossed his arms during his inquisition.

"I'm a big girl, Dem. What's with all the questions? Is this why you came?" she asked, finally annoyed.

Kat busied herself while she put her groceries away. She suddenly felt ashamed of how she lived. She had thought they were doing well, but Demetry's disapproving tone made her question her decision to move to Boston.

Demetry looked around him and then finally directly at Kat. She knew he was disappointed. It was obvious he didn't approve of her living situation.

"Sam came to the house. She let herself in and found me sitting in my basement."

"What? How did she get through the front door?"

"I left the door open."

"*What?* You never leave the door open."

"I know. I know. I made a mistake. Anyway, her and I, well, we got into it pretty good. She really wants to know where you are."

"What did you tell her?"

"Nothing. I told her to forget you and that it was over. She threatened to call the police and she threatened to tell your father."

Kat sat down on the chair across from Demetry, trying to consider Sam's motives. Kat had conveniently pushed all thoughts of Sam out of her mind these past few months. She had been too busy falling in love with Charles to give Sam any further consideration or thought. She had assumed that Sam was moving on with her life, hoping that Sam had found herself in a better relationship.

"She's bluffing. She doesn't have the balls."

"Yeah, I agree. I still felt the need to tell you."

"And, you missed me."

"Yeah, I guess I did."

Kat smiled at her old friend. She knew him better than he thought.

"You want a beer, Dem?"

"Sure, Kat." Demetry pulled out a bag of weed and started to roll a joint at the kitchen table. She sat down next to him and handed him his beer.

"Feels like old times," she said as she rubbed his arm.

Demetry looked up and stared into her eyes.

"You should come home."

CHAPTER 18

Lucy

I was running, unaware that I was dreaming again. It only became obvious when the sun quickly disappeared behind the horizon and blackness followed, like a solar eclipse before my eyes.

I stopped and stood in the middle of my road. The landscape had changed, adding to my confusion. I was on my street, yet there were no houses. The road was long and wide and seemed to go on forever but to nowhere. I slowly started to jog again. As I ran, scenery started to take place where there once was emptiness.

The pavement beneath me gave way to stone. I was familiar with this stone driveway; it was somewhere I had been before. Trees started to appear and then the house. My grandmother's farmhouse. I continued running, feeling the pleasantries and memories invade my soul. A faint breeze cooled the perspiration beading on my skin. I felt calm and relaxed, enjoying my dream state of mind.

As I turned the bend and continued jogging, I passed the broken down border of fencing lining the driveway. I was starting to feel alarmed, but I tried to push through the anxiety. I ran faster than before, trying to crush the frightened emotions that were surfacing.

I looked to my left along the fencing. A small dog appeared, gentle and kind looking, staring at me as his eyes begged for a treat. I stopped and bent down to pet the little beast. I turned to my right and saw, through the trees, Jack walking dressed in his football uniform and helmet.

"Jack!" I yelled, as he continued to walk away from me.

I stood and backed away from the dog, listening to the sounds. The dog whimpered in fear, turned, and ran into the woods behind the fencing. I started my run again, unsure of the noise, hoping to catch up to Jack. I searched for his figure through the trees, catching glimpses of his soiled uniform. I looked toward the farmhouse. Dogs started to appear and litter the front porch, emerging from the windows and along the barn stables. German Shepherds, Rottweilers, and Pitbulls. My heart was racing. I could hear the barking clearer now, the angry growling and aggression becoming more pronounced as I ran closer to the house.

I had the dogs' attention. I decided I shouldn't run, that they may want to run after me, but I wanted to find Jack.

I stood in the middle of the yard and looked up at the second floor window of the farmhouse. Sarah stared down at me. She looked nervous, her eyes wide with curiosity. I stood still and stared at her. I lifted my hand to her, wanting to wave, trying to reach out to her. I could see Sarah's eyes, her smile fading as I saw the wolf-man appear from behind her. He stared down at me, his face gloating as he began to shut the window blinds, disappearing with Sarah behind the curtains.

I moved behind the house, my heart torn between Sarah and Jack, my body trembling, my hands shaking as I felt desperate to help, not sure who to help first. I turned the corner into the backyard and saw Jack, standing still underneath the plum tree. I watched as the plums began to fall around him, smashing on the ground, the smell of sweet juice filling the air. He appeared to be lost, unsure of the woods and his surroundings.

"Jack, Jack…I'm here…I'm coming," I yelled as I ran to reach him. He continued to walk into the woods, disappearing behind the trees, not looking back.

"Jack, wait! Why are you leaving me?" I asked breathlessly. He went on.

I threw myself to the ground and screamed for him, my voice stinging my strained throat, my vocal attempts lost to the trees up above me. I could feel my knees burn as I scraped them against the rugged earth beneath me. The birds flew from their branches, screeching sounds of commotion, while I sobbed, "Why, why aren't you answering me?" I began to grab at the ground, hurtling small stones and twigs into the air at his direction. I covered my face with dirty hands while my tears streamed down my cheeks. I didn't understand why. How could he hurt me so deeply?

The dogs surrounded me. I looked up from my position; I knew they wanted to eat me—they were thin, ratty, and hungry looking. Their fierce growling rang in my ears as they crouched toward the ground, getting ready to pounce on my vulnerable body. I closed my eyes tight. I envisioned myself safe, back on my street in front of my house in my neighborhood, running.

I shot up in bed, sweat pouring down my neck and back. My pillowcase was soaked with moisture. I shook myself from the dream and frantically opened my eyes.

I took a deep breath and slowly calmed my shaking. I remembered everything as my heart felt an emptiness that I recognized.

Jack.

CHAPTER 19

Lucy

Amelia and I walked hand-in-hand down the long, manicured driveway lined with lanterns and beautiful stone walls.

"Are you sure this is the right place, Lucy?" Amelia asked.

"This is the address she gave me."

"It's absolutely beautiful." Amelia gazed in awe at her surroundings.

The house was located in the lovely historical section of town. I felt out of place among the estate and its beautiful lush gardens and rock walls.

As I approached the massive home, my mind was telling me to turn back and leave, find another method for gaining information. My instinct pressed me forward.

Amelia and I walked to the front door. I lifted the centuries-old doorknocker and banged it twice. Amelia looked at me, uncertain of her decision to accompany me to meet Anna.

"It'll be alright, Amelia," I said to reassure her.

"This place is giving me the creeps," she said.

"It's just your imagination getting the best of you. Anna seemed perfectly nice on the phone. If things get strange, just give me the sign and we're out of here. Okay?"

"I'll tell you I'm not feeling well; that will be my cue," Amelia stated.

The massive door started to open, and behind it, a short and plump housemaid stood to greet us. "Miss Anna is waiting for you," she said abruptly.

I turned to look at Amelia. I thought she might pee her pants.

Anna quickly appeared from behind the housemaid and introduced herself.

"Hello, Lucy," she said kindly. She reached out her delicate hand to shake mine.

"Hi Anna. This is my friend Amelia. I hope you don't mind that I brought her along with me."

"Hello, Amelia. No, I don't mind at all. Please come in, girls. Welcome to my home." Anna stood aside as we entered the enormous hallway.

"You have a beautiful house, Anna," Amelia said.

"This home has been in my family for over a hundred years. My great-great grandfather purchased this home, and it's been handed down ever since."

"It's stunning, almost magical," I commented.

Anna smiled kindly. "Can I get you girls something to drink?"

"No, thank you," Amelia stated.

"How about some water?" Anna asked, looking at me.

I didn't want to be rude. "Sure," I said.

"Great. Please, take a seat in the living room and I'll be right back with our drinks."

Amelia and I walked through the grand hallway toward the living room. The noises of our shoes echoed off the walls as we made our way over the marble tiled floor. We entered the living room and gently sat on the beautiful, cream-colored Victorian couches situated in the middle. I gazed up at the twenty-foot ceilings. I admired the beautiful details and trim, the crystal glass chandeliers hanging elegantly from the open space up above. The floor-to-ceiling windows were breathtaking. The living room, beautifully decorated as if out of a magazine article.

We could hear Anna quickly approaching down the hall as she entered the room with a tray full of drinks and snacks.

"Please, help yourselves if you're hungry," she said as she sat across from us in a chair.

"Thank you. You're very sweet," I said.

Anna stared at me briefly. She took a sip of water before she began to speak.

"I'm really glad you decided to call me, Lucy." She turned and addressed Amelia. "I want to start by saying how sorry I am for your loss, Amelia. I understand that you knew the child who drowned at the pool?"

Amelia's eyes were wide with attentiveness as she nodded her head.

"You tried to help her, is that correct?"

Amelia nodded again. She reached into her purse and pulled out several tissues and gripped them fiercely in her hand. I reached over and rubbed her back as she looked forward at Anna. I knew if Amelia tried to speak, her voice would crack. She was still very emotional over the tragedy.

Anna sat back in her chair and closed her eyes. I watched her as she summoned strength or information, I wasn't sure, but something was happening and I didn't want to miss it.

Anna opened her eyes again. "The child's name, was it Peanuts?" Anna asked as she made a funny face. It was an odd name.

Amelia chuckled. "Her name was Penny, but I called her Peanuts. Penny Peanuts. Get it?"

I knew Amelia thought her nickname was clever. I smiled at her silliness.

Anna closed her eyes again. "And did you take her places? She keeps showing me ice cream. Does that make any sense?"

"Yes!" Amelia cried. "Once a week, her mother would ask me to take her for an ice cream cone so her brother can go to his swimming lesson."

Anna smiled as she leaned forward and took Amelia's hand. "Penny, she really enjoyed you. I get the sense that you were close. She would go anywhere with you."

"Yes, she would. She liked to follow me around the pool and ask me questions about this or that. She was so sweet and adorable. I tried to help her, I tried…." Amelia's voice cracked.

"You can't blame yourself, Amelia. There were a lot of kids at the pool that day."

"She was playing a game with the other children. They were taking turns holding their breath under the water. One child was counting. The one who held their breath the longest won. I didn't think anything was wrong." Amelia sobbed, releasing her emotions.

"There was one child there. He put pressure on her, to be better. To be the best," Anna stated.

"Yes…it's her brother. He constantly pushed her, teased her, and forced her into bad situations."

Anna nodded. "She wants you to know it wasn't your fault. Do you understand? It wasn't your fault."

Amelia dried her eyes before she tried to speak again. "I feel so guilty," she croaked.

Anna stood to give Amelia a hug. "You did all you could do."

I watched them as they embraced. Amelia tried to gather her emotions and absorb what Anna was telling her. I handed Amelia my glass of water as she sat back down in her chair.

"Thank you," she said as she took the water.

I looked back at Anna who was staring at me intently.

"Would you mind taking a walk with me?" Anna asked.

I looked at Amelia to make sure she would be all right on her own.

"I'm fine, you can go. I know you have questions," Amelia said. "I really appreciate your help, Anna. I feel better knowing she's all right. I wanted to tell her I was sorry."

"She can hear you, she's listening. You can speak to her and her spirit will hear you," Anna said softly as she held Amelia's hand.

Amelia's face relaxed as she looked around the room and outside of the large windows. "Would you mind if I wander around and take a mini tour of your home while you and Lucy talk?" Amelia asked.

"Absolutely. Feel free to explore. We won't be long," Anna stated.

Anna stood and I followed her through the living room doors and outside onto a private patio. I looked back at Amelia and she waved to me, shyly, unsure of what to do. Anna walked past the crystal blue pool and along a brick walkway until we reached a small sunroom. The room was situated in the middle of the garden with beautiful rose bushes climbing trellises surrounding it. A hummingbird rapidly flitted from bush to bush. I could hear the light flow of water coming from a concrete fountain located at the far end of the garden.

"This is absolutely the most peaceful and quaint garden I've ever seen," I said.

"Thank you, Lucy." Anna smiled. "I think you will learn, when you have the gift of intuition, peace and tranquility is very important. It's essential to surround yourself in comfort."

I followed Anna as she stepped into the small sunroom. A ceiling fan hung from the rafters. Soft, soothing music played in the background. A table and one chair occupied the space in the center of the area. The room was simply decorated, perfectly serene. The pool and patios and beautiful gardens stretched out beyond the bay windows.

"Have a seat on the table, Lucy."

The table was like an exam room table. Big enough to lie on, but small and compact. I hopped up and situated myself while Anna walked around the room, saying prayers and blessings quietly. I watched her as she went through her ritual. She glanced and smiled at me.

"You're so curious," she said. "You can hardly wait."

I smiled shyly. "I just don't understand some things. I'm very anxious to get answers."

"Ah, yes. Well, your mother has a very strong spirit. I feel her; she's here with us. Sarah. Is that correct?"

"Yes. She visits me every night. She touches me."

Anna stopped walking and took a serious look at me.

"She touches you? You can feel her?"

"Yes, every night."

"Well, that's very interesting. Oftentimes, when a spirit hasn't settled or passed over to the other side, they return to their loved ones. They are looking for closure. You've heard of hauntings, I'm sure?"

"Yes, of course."

"It's like that, Lucy. A spirit can haunt the living in many ways. It's weird to feel a touch. It's more common to see a quick glimpse of a shadow or an image. Many people aren't even aware that it's happening. Lay down on the table, dear. I'm going to cover your eyes and I want you to relax."

I lay back on the table. Anna covered my eyes softly with a mask and laid a light blanket over my body. The sound of the music and the soft flow of water in the background was mesmerizing. I could hear Anna walking around the table. I could feel her hands hovering over my body, the heat bouncing off my legs.

"You're so confused. I feel it all over."

"It's been a tough year."

"Your mother, she felt tortured. She agonized over her children. She had severe amounts of anxiety."

I nodded, not sure if I was supposed to answer her. I listened as she continued.

"Her childhood is concerning. She shows me tears, lots of tears. Do you know anything about her life as a child?"

"I never asked her about her childhood. I always assumed it was a happy one. I don't really know."

"Who is Julia?"

"My sister."

"She knows things."

Hmm...that's interesting. "What kind of things?" I asked.

"I sense that she's keeping a secret. I can't tell you what it is, it's not clear. Your father, he needs to find strength. You may need to be stern with him, to snap him out of his depression. You can't let him retreat from his family. Does he spend a lot of time in a garage?"

"Yes." I laughed as I nodded, agreeing with her.

"I can see it. I see the tools and dust that surround him. The anxiety you feel, it's normal. The more you understand your thoughts and visions, the less anxious you will feel when you receive them."

"What about the dreams?" I asked.

"Dreams are very difficult to interpret."

"I see my mother, but she's a child."

"That may have something to do with her childhood. Again, I feel that there's something wrong there. You may need to figure that out. You may have to ask your relatives. Secrets are very common among families." Anna continued to walk around the table. "I was drawn to you at the pool that day. Your instincts are very strong. The interpretation of signs and dreams are a gift and it takes practice. It doesn't happen overnight. Your mother is here; she keeps saying you were her favorite." Anna started to laugh. "She's really persistent...you were her favorite."

I laughed. "I tried to help her, that's all."

"It meant everything to her. Having you made her difficult life a little easier."

"I'm glad I could make her happy."

"Who is Jack?" she asked.

My stomach sank to my feet as a warm flush of heat rapidly spread throughout my body. *How does she know these things?*

"He's nobody," I said with disdain.

"Hmm," Anna replied. "Don't be so harsh, Lucy. People make mistakes."

I nervously rubbed my feet together. The simple mention of Jack's name made my chest burn . The pain I felt continued to linger at the bottom of my stomach, my mind unwilling to accept and feel his rejection. I shoved it down deep, as deep as it could go.

"Who's Kathy or Kathryn?"

"Kathryn is my other sister."

"She's unsettled. I get a sense that there are eyes on her. Someone is watching her."

"What do you mean eyes?" I asked. "I don't understand."

"Well, pictures appear in my head and I have to interpret them. When I see a pair of eyes, I've learned over time that it's maybe a love interest, or it's actually someone watching that person. In Kathryn's case, my sense is telling me that someone is watching her. She may feel it too or be aware of it because I feel that her soul is unsettled."

"Oh, I see." I thought about Anna's words and my sister. I needed to call her, make sure she was okay. "What about dogs? I have these dreams and I'm always confronted with angry, vicious dogs."

"Dogs are tricky. Dogs could mean protection, or they could indicate danger. Again, interpretation is difficult to the untrained. Keep your thoughts clear, Lucy, and keep your eyes open to suggestion. Follow your instincts; they are very strong."

Anna took the mask off my eyes and I slowly sat up.

"How do you feel?" she asked.

"Tired."

Anna laughed. "It's very draining, isn't it?"

"Exhausting!"

"Come, let's go rescue Amelia. The poor thing is suffering through my housemaid's old family photos."

We walked quietly back toward the house and sure enough, Agnes was showing Amelia her family album. Amelia stood as soon as she saw me.

"Are we ready to go?" she asked.

"Yes, Amelia, I'm all set."

I turned to Anna as she reached out to embrace me.

"Stay in touch, Lucy. I'm here to help you."

"Thank you, Anna. I will."

I turned and grabbed on to Amelia's arm and we walked quickly through the loud front hall and out of the stately front door. I was glad I came. Anna was very helpful. I understood now. Things were a little clearer.

CHAPTER 20

Lucy

I dropped Amelia off at her mother's and drove home quickly. I was late. I knew Mikey had baseball tonight. He would need a snack and a ride to practice. I thought about Anna and her advice. I thought of all the information now, floating around in my head. I wanted to call Julia. I wanted to ask her about my mother. I needed to find out what she knew. I considered calling my grandmother. I didn't know if she would help me. I didn't know if she would be honest.

I pulled into my driveway and spotted my father's car. Mikey was sitting on the stoop waiting for me. He was noticeably irritated.

"Hey Mikey…I'm sorry I'm late."

"If I'm late for practice, they won't let me start in tomorrow's game," he said, annoyed.

"Where's Dad?" I asked.

"In the house."

"Did you eat anything?"

"I'm not hungry," he said.

I could hear Anna's words in the back of my head regarding my father. This was ridiculous. He couldn't make Mikey a snack before his practice? He couldn't bring him to practice? Mikey needed a man around to support him. He didn't need me; he needed his father.

I walked into the house and looked for my father. I found him lying on the couch, half asleep.

"Dad!" I yelled. I startled him awake.

"What? Jesus! You scared me." My father jolted into an upright position, rubbing his hands over his face as he looked at me.

"Mikey has practice! He hasn't eaten anything. He'll be starving," I said, disappointed, like I was talking to a child.

135

"I thought you were going to bring him?"

"Why not *you*, Dad? Are you too busy right now, taking a nap? Why didn't you bring him?"

My father heaved himself off the couch. "I guess I'll bring him then," he spat.

He walked past me into the kitchen. I stopped and grabbed his arm.

"He needs you, Dad. We all do. I'm eighteen; I can't stay here forever. You need to start participating in our lives."

He nodded at me, accepting my words with no rebuttal. He grabbed his keys and walked outside. I stared out of the window as he talked to Mikey.

"Come on, buddy, I'll drive you to practice. I'd like to see how your hitting is coming along."

"Really? Oh great! Thanks, Dad!" Mikey hurried to my father's car, excited for the new change in arrangements.

I sat down on the kitchen stool and thought to myself.

That felt good!

CHAPTER 21

Sam

Sam watched the great rescue unfolding on the street. She watched as Demetry assaulted the man harassing Kat. She watched how grateful Kat was, how happy she was to see him. It was so obvious, how much Demetry loved her. She didn't know whom he thought he was fooling. He was such an arrogant jerk. It was so obvious.

Sam pulled her dark hooded sweatshirt up over her head and tried to conceal her face. She looked around her at all the trash littered on the road. She wanted to avoid the people walking down the sidewalk. She tried to avoid their eyes. She could be the next victim being harassed on the street and she didn't have a Demetry to run in and save the day for her. No one would care if she went missing. No one would care.

Kat, who does she think she is? How dare she take advantage of her? Sam could see the two of them walking in front of her at a safe distance. Kat's smiling; she looks so relieved and happy. She has her arm around Demetry's arm and they're walking quickly, hurrying to get somewhere. He's probably going to fuck her. They probably can't wait to be alone together. They're so disgusting.

The thought of the two of them made her sick.

She needed to know where Kat lived. She followed them around the corner to a rundown brick apartment building. She watched them as they climbed the battered concrete stoop and opened her apartment door. They disappeared beyond the entrance, closing out the world behind them.

What was she doing here? Why does she live here? Sam didn't understand what was happening with Kat. She looked around the area. This was no place for anyone to live, let alone Kat. Why would she leave Demetry's?

There was only one thing that she could do. She needed to find a place to stay. She needed to watch over Kat, make sure that she was all right. She didn't want anything bad to happen to her Kat. Kat needed her. It was what she would want.

Sam looked up at the building next door. She glanced at the sign in the window.

APARTMENT FOR RENT.

Perfect!

CHAPTER 22

Lucy

I called my grandmother and asked her if she wanted to go to lunch. She instead invited me to her house and told me she would make me food. She was so happy that I called her and was eager to do something special for me, anything. I told her I would be over by noon.

I thought over my strategy, to get information out of her. I would like more pictures of my great grandma's farm. I wish she were still alive. She might have been more helpful. If I could get Grandma to reminisce about my mother and her mother, maybe I could get somewhere with her. That was my plan, anyway. My backup plan was to contact Julia. My second backup plan was to contact my crazy aunt. I'm leaving that plan for last because it's definitely a last resort.

Jessica and Kaylan were getting old enough to keep an eye on Mikey. I allowed them to walk to the town pool and called Amelia to let her know that they would be there today. She would keep an extra eye on them for me. Amelia was in charge of all the camp events now and I was sure she'd sign them up for whatever extra activities she could.

I took a shower and dressed quickly, hoping that I wouldn't change my mind about going to my grandmother's. My mother's history was important to me, but I was also fearful as to what I might find. What happened to my mother? What drove a seemingly normal woman so over the edge in such a short amount of time? It was hard to understand.

As I drove the distance to my grandmother's house, I thought about Jack. I was so angry with myself. Why did I get so attached to him? All those years, wasted, all that energy and worry. I wondered if he'd go to college now. I wondered if he'd stay on the farm. I couldn't bear to talk to him. I couldn't bear to give that boy one more minute of my precious time. Everything I'd ever felt for him, all the worry, concern, and now sadness and hurt. What good did I ever feel? The only time I felt loved was the one and only time we were intimate together, and that lasted only one day. It wasn't enough. I wanted to forget and stop thinking about him.

141

I pushed those negative thoughts out of my mind as I pulled into my grandmother's driveway. I maneuvered down the long path past the large colonial house and parked in the back. It was early enough and my grandmother was out tinkering around in her flower gardens. Otis, my grandmother's springer spaniel, was first to greet me. I kneeled down on the sidewalk and gave the dog my attention. Otis ran around in circles and jumped to lick my face. I yelled and waved at my grandmother to alert her of my arrival. Her hearing wasn't the best and I didn't want to startle her. She smiled and waved and then continued the task of trimming her rose bushes.

Oh brother, I think this is going to be a long visit. She was in no rush today. She was going to keep me here for as long as she could. I decided to walk into the house and waited for her there. She would eventually join me when she was ready.

As I walked into the kitchen, I noticed my mother's picture on a desk with candles surrounding it. Prayer candles. A small shrine, I guess. I looked at the photograph. In it, my mother was young and beautiful. This must be her high school photograph. I could tell by the hairstyle, it was definitely outdated. My mother's eyes were serious and I got the sense that she was standing here, in the kitchen with me. I suddenly felt nervous to pry, nervous and uncomfortable. Sometimes family secrets were secret for a good reason. Who was I to try to understand them, but then I thought about my mother's visits. She definitely had a purpose for me. She needed something from me; I just needed to understand what that was.

"Mama, give me strength," I prayed.

"Strength for what, sweetheart?" my grandmother asked.

"Oh! Hi, Gram! I didn't hear you come in." Jesus Christ, she scared me half to death.

"Hi, dear. I just needed to finish pruning those damn rose bushes. If I don't cut them back now, they'll take over my garden next year. Would you care for a drink?"

"Sure, that sounds good. I was just saying a prayer at your shrine. My mother's picture, is this her high school photo?"

"I believe it is. It's the only large picture I have of her." My grandmother reached into the cabinet for a glass and poured me a cup of lemonade. I looked around the kitchen. It wasn't as tidy as I remembered it. She had her teacup and a deck of cards placed on the table by her chair. Books upon books were scattered about. My uncle had moved her washer and dryer into the kitchen so she didn't have to use the basement stairs, adding to the clutter. My grandmother was a bit of a hoarder. She

143

collected things, antique dishware and furniture. My mother's death had taken a toll on her. She appeared slow and frail. It couldn't be easy for her, living alone. My grandmother was turning eighty soon. I should come here more often, to help her.

"Hey Gram? Do you have other photos of Mom? Photos of when she was younger, as a child. I'd like to have some of them. We don't have any." I sat at the dining table as my grandmother placed a glass of lemonade in front of me.

"Yes, of course I do. They are old photos, black and white pictures. I keep them in boxes upstairs in the attic. The boxes are too big for me to carry, but perhaps you can get them down. I made tuna fish, is that alright?"

"Yes, thank you. I love tuna."

My grandmother continued to make our sandwiches as I sat at the table, considering my next question.

"How are you doing, Gram? Are you okay? I feel horrible about the incident with Dad. I still don't understand why he's so angry."

My grandmother glanced at me. "I'm fine. I know he's under tremendous stress. I've decided not to take it personally."

"Do you know why he's so angry?" I looked at my grandmother. I watched her face, to see if she was nervous.

"I'm not sure what you mean—angry? Of course he's upset and devastated over your mother. We all are. It's understandable."

"It seems to me that there are other issues. I just don't understand what they are."

"Perhaps you should ask him. It would seem more appropriate that you ask him that sort of question. He would be the only one who could answer it." My grandmother handed me my sandwich and sat across from me.

"Yeah, maybe you're right. Thank you, Gram, this looks great." I started to eat my sandwich. I looked over my bread to ensure that it wasn't moldy. I loved my grandmother but older people liked to hold on to their groceries. I closed my eyes and an overwhelming sense of exhaustion filled my soul. I could sense that my grandmother was stalling. I could see my mother nodding her head up and down, an indication that she wanted me to keep pushing. I wasn't going to get the information that I needed from my grandmother unless I was forceful. I finished my sandwich quickly and cleaned my plate at the sink.

"Gram? Can I ask you a question?"

145

"Sure, honey."

"What do you think happened to Mom?"

My grandmother sat in her chair and stared at me blankly. She inhaled deeply and cleared her throat. She sat back and paused to close her eyes. When she opened them, tears streamed down her face as she quickly wiped them with her napkin. She began to speak, her voice strained and twisted from the unexpected emotions.

"I loved your mother; I miss her dearly," she started. "When you are a grown woman, Lucy, you will understand things. You will understand that life isn't perfect and that sometimes, bad things happen. Sometimes, things aren't in your control, as much as you try." My grandmother stopped and stood to clear her plate.

"I'm leaving, Lucy. I'm moving down south with your aunt."

I looked at my grandmother, shocked as she spoke. I thought we were starting to have a real conversation. I thought I was getting somewhere with her.

"When did you decide this? Were you even going to say goodbye?"

"You kids don't need me now. Your father has made that clear to me. I can't stay in this big house alone anymore. It's too much; I'm getting too old. I'm going to move to Florida. Your uncle is buying the house."

"So, that's it? You're just going to leave?"

"I'm sorry, Lucy."

I stared at my grandmother in disbelief. "I don't know what to say. I hope you'll be happy there." I stood to embrace my grandmother. I hugged her tightly, thinking that I may never see her again. I kissed her on her cheek and held her hand. I wish she had more courage, courage to be honest about my mother's life.

"I think I'll head upstairs now, if that's okay."

"Sure, Lucy. Take something, anything that you think you may like up there."

"Thank you, that would be nice, Gram."

"Can you do me a favor, Lucy? While you're up in the attic, can you bring down the braided rugs I have at the top of the staircase and drag them outside for me? I'd like to air them out and give them a good pounding. I'm sure they're layered with dust."

I heard her continue to talk about the rugs and how my uncle was supposed to bring them down for her, how lazy he was, how he drank too much. I quietly walked out of the kitchen and yelled, "No problem!" as I quickly climbed the layered staircase to the second floor of the house.

I stopped midway and briefly glanced out over the window seat that overlooked the backyard. I remembered as a young kid sitting on the cozy window seat, reading my books and coloring with my crayons. The double windows opened to the back of the house, beautiful but dangerous. Any small child could easily climb on the seat and fall over the unprotected windowsill. In fact, I'm pretty sure Kathryn fell once. The image of Kathryn falling forced its way into my mind, but I quickly pushed it back. I didn't have time for memories now. I wanted to find the pictures.

I continued climbing the staircase until I reached the second floor. The old house creaked and spoke to me through its wooden floors and plastered walls. I walked down the narrow hallway until I approached the door to the attic. I carefully opened the unused door and glanced up the stairs to the abandoned upper floor, my heart racing, my nerves getting the best of me, placing fear into my soul, for I hadn't been in my grandmother's attic since I was a child. Back then, it was a fun place to play hide and seek and look for buried treasure. Back then, I would have had my siblings with me, running, jumping, hiding. Now, I was alone. It felt foolish to say that I was scared, but I was.

I continued forward and started my climb up the stairs. Several steps were missing or broken from the staircase so I climbed carefully. As I approached the top, I could see the large braided rugs my grandmother wanted me to carry down for her. I pulled on one to try to move it. *Is she out of her mind?* These rugs were extremely heavy. I took a deep breath and continued to look around the attic for the boxes. As I walked through the large space, it struck me that I may never find what I'm looking for. I'm not even sure what it is I'm trying to find. I hoped I'd understand it when I saw it, but I didn't know.

I could feel a draft from the attic's ceiling fan as its breeze blew the hair off the back of my neck. I could feel sudden goosebumps moving up and down my arms. This place gave me the creeps.

I took my hand and cleared some of the cobwebs that were hanging from the attic's rafters before I started to look through the boxes. I opened the first set of boxes and looked for the pictures. One by one, I unraveled the cardboard. Dinner plates, glassware, linens, and princess house crystal filled the boxes. Good lord, my dear grandmother needed to have a tag sale.

I pushed those boxes to the back of the room and started on another set. A sense of determination filled my chest as I heard my grandmother walking around the second floor. She yelled up the staircase to see how I was doing. I glanced down at her and gave her a wave. "Doing fine, Gram. I'll be down shortly. Don't walk up here, it's not very safe."

What is it I'm looking for? I walked around looking for other boxes. I read the labels on the cardboard, hoping to save myself some time. I found one box with the word *Photos* written on the side. I opened the box quickly and I could tell immediately that these were old pictures. I riffled through them to make sure and then placed the box near the stairs.

I gave myself one more glance through the attic when I noticed a small chest located in the far corner. The chest looked old and promising. I opened the chest and let the dust settle before I pillaged through the items. I found old books, old linens, and some old maps of Vermont. As I looked closer, I found a small bag of pictures. They were of my great grandmother's farm and there was one of my great grandmother and great grandfather.

Satisfied, I grabbed the box of pictures and made my way downstairs where my grandmother was patiently waiting for me.

"Hey, Gram! There's no way I could carry those rugs down for you. They are way too heavy."

"You people, you can't do anything for me!" My grandmother looked at me, disgusted with my inability to drag hundred-pound rugs down two flights of stairs.

"Sorry, Gram. Thank you for the pictures. Is it okay if I take one of your quilts?"

"Absolutely. I need to clear out some of this clutter. You can think of me on a cold, wintery night." She laughed.

I quickly took the box and moved it into my car and began to say my final goodbye. "Good luck, Gram. Keep in touch," I said as I got into my vehicle.

"I love you," Gram said as she waved. I pulled out of her driveway.

It felt strange to say goodbye as I thought about my grandmother. So many unanswered questions still swarmed around my busy head.

I drove down the road, feeling somewhat accomplished and relieved to have some of my mother's history. What I was going to do with it I didn't know, but for now, I was satisfied.

CHAPTER 23

Lucy

I dumped the box of pictures out on the dining room table. I tried to put them in chronological order according to the year. I removed all the pictures of the people I didn't recognize. I focused mainly on my mother's pictures and her siblings along with my great grandmother's pictures and her farm. There was one picture of my great grandfather. I stared at it. I tried to feel something for the picture, but I felt nothing. He didn't look into the camera; he looked down at the ground. It wasn't a good picture. I recognized the photos with my uncle and my grandmother along with her sisters. The children's faces were serious and staged. It looked like a professional picture, not an impromptu one.

When I finished organizing the pictures, I placed them in a photo album to keep them orderly and safe from destruction. I heard my father's car pull into the driveway. I quickly shut the photo album and ran up the stairs to place it under my bed for future reference. I didn't want my father asking questions. I didn't want him to be angry.

My anxiety, it was heavy. I had an uneasy feeling. I needed to exercise. I grabbed my sneakers and went for a run. All I ever seemed to do is run lately. Thank god for exercise.

CHAPTER 24

Jack

I missed her. I thought of her constantly. I knew she hated me. I thought it was a good idea to break it off with her, so I could move forward. I thought if I ended it, my life would get easier. It wasn't working. I still needed her. She still dominated my thoughts and my mind. I contemplated going to her, jumping in my truck and driving the long distance to see her. I could be there by noon tomorrow, but I was afraid that it was too late.

She would never forgive me.

I can't even forgive myself.

Stupid…stupid…stupid.

CHAPTER 25

Lucy

My family gathered in the driveway to say goodbye to Thomas. His car was packed, his bags were full, and he was excited to start the upcoming school year.

Amelia stood by my side with tears in her eyes. We waved frantically to Tommy as he pulled out of our street.

I placed my arm around Amelia and we walked back into the house, relieved for it to be over. Amelia had to excuse herself and retreat to my bedroom for some time. She was overly emotional. I felt sorry for her. She had a rough summer between my family, her job, and my brother. We'd both like to rush through this year and move on with our lives. Amelia at least had a plan for her future. Her plan was to follow my brother wherever he may go. Eventually they would settle down, marry, and have a family. I was happy for them. They were in love and extremely devoted to one another. I couldn't have dreamed of a better sister-in-law.

My father's behavior had gotten better. He seemed to have taken my advice about keeping himself busy with the kids, instead of hiding himself in the garage alone. Being busy with my siblings has been my only source of joy and distraction from the depression. I knew my father needed us.

My father walked into the kitchen and sat down at the counter with a reserved look over his face. I decided to start lunch and watched him closely.

"What's wrong, Dad?"

My father glanced up at me.

"It's weird. Watching your kids grow up and leave the house. Everything moves so quickly. Soon enough, I'll be alone in this big house with no one. It scares me to be alone. I had always envisioned your mother and I enjoying retirement, taking care of grandkids and starting a whole new life experience together. That won't happen now."

My father paused and looked down at his hands, acceptance registering on his face.

I tried to imagine what he must have been feeling. I felt so sorry for him, I wanted to help him but there was nothing I could do.

"Do you ever consider that you may find someone again, another woman?"

"I can't possibly think about that now." My father stood, walked around the counter, and gave me an unexpected hug. "I just want to enjoy you kids while I have you here. You kids are growing and will be moving on sooner than later. I want to be a part of it; I want to spend as much time with you as I can, while I can."

I looked at my father, shocked and relieved at his words. I suddenly felt some hope for the future. I suddenly felt support from my father. It was a comforting feeling, to hear him speak.

"Let me make you lunch, Lucy. You've done so much for me; I really appreciate you, honey. Thank you."

"Are you sure?"

"Yes. Go relax and I'll call you when it's ready."

I walked out of the kitchen slowly, looking back at my father, waiting for him to change his mind.

He started to laugh. "I'm not helpless, you know! I do know how to make lunch!"

I smiled at him deeply. "Thank you, Dad."

I thought about Amelia. I tried to give her some space to mourn the departure of my brother, but after a few hours, I thought maybe I should check on her. I slowly cracked my bedroom door open. Amelia lay on my bed with her face shoved into my pillow, like a small child would when placed in time out. Her little body was stretched along the length of my mattress. I had to laugh.

I sat down next to her and placed my hand on her back. I could hear the soft sobs escape her as she tried to ignore my presence.

"Are you okay?" I asked.

Amelia released a deep sigh as she shook her head.

"It's going to be alright, Amelia. Maybe we can go to Boston next weekend and visit."

"Can you hand me a tissue?" Amelia asked.

I stood and walked into the bathroom to grab some toilet paper. I smiled to myself. She's so cute when she's vulnerable.

"Here you go. Can I get you anything else?"

Amelia rolled over and looked at me with scared, uncertain eyes. I got the sense that she was about to say something important. I found it a little unusual and out of character for her to be so devastated over my brother's leaving. She knew she would see him again. It was only a two-hour drive. She was far more confident than that.

Amelia sat up and grabbed my arm desperately.

"Ouch, geez. You're acting really strange. I think you need to get it together."

"Lucy?" Amelia's eyes filled with tears as her voice quivered beneath her breath. I was instantly nervous for her; she was so upset. What was going on?

"What is it, Amelia? You're scaring me."

"I'm *pregnant*!"

CHAPTER 26

Lucy

I turned slowly while my body lay softly on the ground in the forest, surrounded by daffodils. Daffodils were one of my mother's favorite flowers. I floated above the forest floor, looking up through the massive trees, catching scattered glimpses of the sun and blue sky. I felt so peaceful. This was a dream, I knew, and I was relaxed among its serenity and aura. I closed my eyes and felt the weightlessness of my body. I moved my arms slowly like I was swimming in the ocean, while flower petals appeared to float all around my body. I could smell the sweet aroma of the blossoms as they filled my senses with joy.

I heard my name, softly at first.

"Lucy," she singingly called to me. "Lucy, open your eyes," she whispered. Her voice was delicate and sweet, so safe. I didn't want to open my eyes. I didn't want the dream to change. "Lucy...come, take my hand."

I opened my eyes.

It was Sarah, sweet little Sarah. She hovered over me above the forest floor with her hand reaching out for mine. She was angelic in her white, floating nightgown blowing softly around her petite body. She laughed, a child's laugh. The sweet sound of a giggle you only heard when little girls played.

I reached for her and we locked hands. She pulled me gently to her and we floated together, throughout the forest, in and out of trees and above the land. We watched each other and smiled, giggling secretly as we made our way like children. We stared at each other knowingly as our minds seemed to communicate without words.

Sarah led me carefully. She showed me the beautiful visions of the forest. She took me to the waterfalls; we visited the bear dens and the fields of rabbits and deer. It was lovely and I wanted to stay here with her. I wanted to be with Sarah, forever.

Sarah and I took refuge on a large tree branch overlooking the watering hole, where the animals would come to rest and drink. We sat on the bough, our legs dangling from the limb, holding hands. I felt such peace with Sarah. We took turns throwing acorns into the water. I could hear myself laughing, my voice distant and unfamiliar. Gentle childhood memories ran through my thoughts as I glanced down at the water. Happy, thoughtful memories of my siblings and I playing games on a warm summer day. Happy, thoughtful reminders of my mother.

I glanced up through the trees and watched the sky change. It began to rain, the gentle drops of moisture refreshing on our delicate skin. I closed my eyes and lifted my chin so I could enjoy the summer shower, when a sudden clap of thunder made me jump and shook the earth and the tree we sat in.

As in all my dreams, blackness replaced the sunshine. Lightning spread across the sky in sharp spears of fluorescent light. Sudden fear and anxiety superseded the peace and happiness.

That was when I noticed it. That was when my heart stopped beating. When the air in my chest would get caught up in my throat and began to resist me.

A body. A human body floating slowly down the small stream and into the watering hole. I tried to speak, but my voice was stilled. Sarah continued to laugh and giggle and float about the tree's branches.

I closed my eyes and I was instantly in the water, rushing to help the floating person. It was my sister Kathryn floating toward me, lifeless. I ran through the water, screaming her name, trying desperately to reach her, but the water was heavy and it pulled me the opposite direction.

I looked toward Sarah, begging her to help me, but she only giggled. *This is only a dream. This is not real.* I closed my eyes and prayed. I stood in the water as it rushed past me down the stream. I could see Kathryn's body ahead of me, coming my way. If I stood still and waited for her, she would come to me and I could save her. I watched eagerly as her body rose and fell over the rivers rocks and boulders, the waves and currents moving her forward. Her body was face down in the water.

I readied myself to grab hold of her before she swiftly passed me by. I grabbed her arm and the body turned on me and grabbed my shoulders, quickly pulling me under the water's surface. Shocked, I opened my eyes to see its face. The face, not of Kathryn, but of the man, the man with the doglike features.

I struggled under the water to break free as he wrestled me against the rocks. The man ripped and clawed at my clothing, physically shoving my face under water, again and again. I might die here. I thought I was safe and protected, but he's fooled me.

He wanted Sarah for himself. I gasped for air as my face would surface briefly, screaming for Sarah, only to be pulled down again.

I heard in the back of my mind, *He's afraid of you.*

I remembered as a kid the encouraging words my mother would often say: "Be brave, Lucy; have courage."

I opened my eyes quickly and glared at the man trying to kill me. With inhuman strength, I found my footing on the bed of the stream and shot myself out of the water and into the cool, crisp forest air. I slowly gathered myself and hovered over the man flailing around in the water below me, trying desperately to find me. I shot back down at him with my fists engaged and I hit him directly in the chest, sending him flying across the riverbank. The man's image disappeared into thin air as he hit the edge of a heavy boulder, leaving nothing behind but water droplets and space. His nasty scent remained, a horrible reminder of his wretchedness.

I heard a giggle. I looked up and saw Sarah, staring down at my drenched body. She floated to me and grabbed my hand and kissed it. She looked at me and began to speak.

"You are strong, Lucy. You must always remember your strength."

Sarah disappeared and then I closed my eyes.

When I opened them again, I was in my bed, safe and sound. I shook my head and steadied my thoughts. I tried to calm my breathing. I couldn't live like this. I couldn't keep fighting demons in my sleep while trying to solve my mother's constant rhymes and riddles. This was exhausting. I needed to call Julia to get some answers. I needed to get to the bottom of these dreams. I wanted to quiet my mother's soul so she could rest in peace.

Warm and cozy feelings began to envelop me along with my new attitude of arrogant strength and power. I smiled as I lay back down to sleep.

I was strong. I was definitely strong.

CHAPTER 27

Kathryn

Kat felt so empty after Demetry left Boston for home. She begged him to stay the night, but he said he had things to do. He asked her several times to come with him. She was tempted, very tempted. She could imagine herself sitting in Demetry's kitchen, shooting the breeze and feeling safe and secure back in her old life.

She couldn't leave Charles. He would never forgive her. This was her life now. She was a woman of change and experience. She was enjoying their time together. She was a fisherman's girlfriend, and the hard rugged lifestyle suited her. She had a lot of respect for Charles and his chosen career path. He did what he loved.

She thought about Charles as she made dinner for the boys. It was late, almost 10:00, but she knew that they would be hungry. Time didn't matter when you were on the boat. She missed him now that she didn't go to work with him every day. She wondered if she should get a different job; perhaps she needed to talk to him about that. Waiting in the apartment all day for Charles and Jimmy to come home was driving her crazy. She knew what he would say: "We're leaving in a few weeks; why get a job now?"

"You need to let me back on the boat," she'll argue. It was so boring, being alone. Maybe now would be a good time for her to go home for a couple of weeks, before they headed down south. That was a great idea! She could go home, say goodbye, and spend some time with her family.

A smile spread across her face as she thought about it. It was exactly what she wanted to do.

The apartment buzzer rang, which was her sign that the boys were home. She hit the intercom button so the main door would open, allowing them to come up to the apartment. The boys were exhausted, dirty, and hungry. She greeted Charles with an excited hug and kiss as he entered the door of their little bungalow. Jimmy high-fived her and began to tell her all about their day, and the massive tuna they caught. The boys quickly sat

168

at the table and she served them their dinner, beef stew and cornbread. She couldn't keep her eyes off Charles, his face unshaven and his hair a mess. His manly and strong appearance always impressed her. She hoped Jimmy had something to do tonight. She and Charles could use some privacy, and she really wanted to talk with him about going home.

Jimmy excused himself from the dinner table and stated that he needed to take a shower.

"Going anywhere special tonight, Jimmy?" she asked. *Please say yes. Please say yes.*

"I don't want to stick around here all night, watching you too gawk at each other," he teased. He quickly moved around the apartment, gathering his things.

"Stop it! We do not." She grinned. Charles glanced at her and their eyes met. Her heart skipped a beat, when he casually looked at her that way.

Jimmy disappeared down the hallway and Kat quickly busied herself at the kitchen sink with the dishes. She could hear Charles push his chair away from the table as he suddenly approached her from behind and put his dish in the sink. He lingered at her back and he whispered in her ear, "You look amazing tonight." He softly kissed the side of her neck and placed his hand under her shirt to cup her breast.

Kat stepped back slightly to give him full access as he continued to kiss her gently. She could smell the odor of the ocean breeze mixed in with the smelly fish, but it was a comforting smell. Her senses had become immune to it.

He quickly turned her around and kissed her passionately while he pressed her against the kitchen counter. Her thoughts about going home suddenly escaped her mind as Charles' hands began to roam all over her body, leaving her breathless, mindless.

"God, Kat, all I could think about was you today," he whispered.

She moaned quietly while he spoke to her, lost in the sexual feelings of want and desire. She heard Jimmy singing in the bathroom as he got ready for his night. She couldn't wait for him to leave.

Charles stopped himself before things got out of control. "Why don't you get ready for me in our room? I want to clean the stench off me before I get ready to fuck you properly," he said, gritting his teeth.

Oh my god. She could hardly restrain herself. Her heart was racing and her legs were shaking. She slipped out of Charles' embrace and walked quickly into their bedroom. She turned on the lamp and began to light the few candles she had scattered about on their nightstand. She looked at herself in the mirror, then tossed her hair back in a messy bun and ripped open her dresser drawer. She took out the nightgown she purchased last week at a lingerie sale. It fit her perfectly. The coral-colored satin garment fit snugly around her breasts, pushing them up, while the soft floating material covered her ass just below her cheeks. She looked at herself in the mirror. She felt sexy with her tanned skin and blonde highlights. She hoped Charles would appreciate this.

She could hear Jimmy yelling goodbye as he left the apartment. She was so grateful for this time with Charles. He had been so busy and tired lately. He worked so hard.

She ran back into the kitchen and grabbed a bottle of wine and two glasses. As she made her way back into the bedroom, Charles exited the bathroom and intercepted her in the hallway. His eyes took in her appearance and he stopped her from moving any farther. She stared at his naked chest, the water from the shower still beading off his tanned skin. His arms were strong and muscular from months of working on the boat. Charles removed the wine bottle and glasses from her hands and placed them on the table. Their chests rose and fell as the anticipation of making love built in their minds. Kat grabbed hold of the towel wrapped casually around his waist and pulled him toward her. She reached up and kissed his lips as he quickly picked her up and carried her into their bedroom.

Her mind was racing as Charles placed her carefully on the bed. He hovered over her and whispered, "I love you, Kat. God, I love you."

Tears filled her eyes as she whispered back, "I love you too, Charles." She desperately removed the towel from his waist, revealing his perfectly beautiful body as he began to kiss her neck and her breasts. The thin satin material of her nightgown hardly concealed her swollen nipples as they responded to Charles' aggressive touch.

He settled himself in between her legs, quickly removing her panties with a sharp tear as he held her hands above her head. He entered her harsh and fiercely, sending a ripple of pain and pleasure bolting throughout her body.

"Oh god!" she yelled from the sudden, unexpected assault. Charles continued to move within her body, thrusting harder and harder into her, relentless in his need to be fulfilled.

The satin material of her nightgown was unable to contain her breasts as Charles made love to her. He ripped the material from her skin. She could feel his warm chest against hers, her legs wrapped tightly around his waist as he continued to have his way with her. The pleasure of this man was overwhelming. The internal connection…you could never feel this with a woman.

She could see the gratification cross Charles face as he came closer to releasing himself into her, his assault sending sparks of pleasure to every point of her being. She could no longer hold on to her senses as the orgasmic pleasure overcame her mind and body.

"Charles…god, Charles!" she yelled as she gripped her nails into his biceps, unable to control herself. Charles cried out as her orgasmic flesh suddenly tightened and restricted him. He released himself and collapsed on top of her, their bodies exhausted by their efforts.

Their heavy breathing slowed as they lay together, still connected physically. The sweat caused by the hot summer air clung to their foreheads. She knew that their lovemaking was not over. Charles was insatiable. She moved her hips slightly to feel the man who lay within her, her body still sensitive from orgasm. Charles looked up into her face, responding to her movement.

He moved ever so slowly inside her, forcing himself as deep as he could go, watching her face the entire time. He grabbed one of her legs and held it tightly while her breasts were smashed against his chest, spilling out and around her body.

Slowly he began to move. She closed her eyes and enjoyed him while he took his time with her.

"Are you okay, Kat?" he whispered softly.

"You feel incredible. Don't stop, please don't stop," she begged, her voice barely audible.

"I'm not going to stop, baby. I'm just getting started."

She could feel Charles' erection filling her insides as he grew from the excitement of her touch. Slowly he teased her, in and out, deeper and deeper. It was almost unbearable.

"Can you say the words?" he asked roughly as he took hold of her ass and rolled her on top of him. She screamed from the sudden change in position, her body thrilled by his assertiveness, his aggressiveness. His mouth assaulted her breasts as she leaned over in his face to give him better reign. He pulled on her, biting her painfully. She was dying from pleasure.

She whispered in his ear, "I need you, Charles. I need you desperately. I love you."

Charles was unable to resist her words, but she was in control. She took his arms and held them over his head as she slowly moved herself up and down, her legs squeezing his waist fiercely. She kissed his mouth passionately, pulling at his lips and teasing him with her tongue. Charles moaned deeply, an indication that he was no longer going to tolerate her subtleness.

Quickly, Charles moved her off his body and positioned her so he could take her from behind. He slammed himself into her as hard as he could.

"OH MY GOD!" she screamed.

Again and again, he had his way with her. Squeezing and grabbing at her breasts aggressively, satisfying her with both pleasure and pain. Her mind was spinning, her body on the edge of collapsing. They filled the apartment with bursts of moaning, screams of pleasure and gratification.

They orgasm together, their bodies at last fulfilled by their love and passion.

Charles lied down beside her, his arms wrapped tightly around her. He whispered, "I love you, Kathryn."

"I love you too, Charles."

He slept.

CHAPTER 28

Lucy

Waiting for the doctor to return was torture. I sat close to Amelia in the small, cramped hospital room while she fidgeted with her hands, her eyes still fearful and uncertain. I tried to convince her that she would be fine, that she would make a beautiful mother. I reassured her that my brother would take care of her, support her and be a good father. She still hadn't told him. She was only eight weeks along, but I thought that he should know. I didn't want to put too much pressure on her, but I felt a lot of responsibility now. I was the only one who knew about her condition and I felt a deep concern for her.

"Amelia, you need to mention to the doctor about your morning sickness. You need to tell him how difficult it is for you to keep any food down."

"I will, Lucy. Maybe he can give me something for it. I just feel so awful. I have no energy to do anything."

"I'm sure it will get better. I've been reading that the first few months are the most difficult."

The doctor knocked on the door and let himself into the room. "Hello, Amelia," he said kindly.

"Hi Dr. Jones. This is my friend, Lucy. She's been taking care of me." Amelia smiled at me.

"Hello, Lucy." The doctor grabbed onto a rolling chair and sat down with his medical folder in his hand. "So, I've got the test results back and it's official, you are definitely pregnant." Amelia nodded as she listened to the doctor speak. "I need to ask, do you know who the father is?"

"Of course I do!" Amelia looked shocked and offended by his words.

"The father is my brother, Dr. Jones."

Dr. Jones glanced at me while he was trying to figure out our relationship.

"Amelia is my best friend," I said.

"Well, that's very important. She will need a lot of help and support before and after the baby is born. Where is your brother now?" he asked.

"Thomas is away at college. He lives in Boston. He's unaware of Amelia's condition. I've been trying to convince her that she needs to tell him, but she's afraid." Dr. Jones looked at Amelia with concern and sympathy.

"I know this must be very scary for you. How do you feel, Amelia?"

"Sick. I can't eat anything."

Dr. Jones nodded and took out a prescription pad and started writing.

"This should be temporary, Amelia. Most women experience morning sickness the first few months of pregnancy, but it should subside. It's very important for you to get your nutrition. Try to eat whatever you can manage to keep down. I'm going to give you a prescription for vitamins, as well as for your nauseous stomach." Dr. Jones handed me the prescriptions. "I'm trusting that you could fill these for her?"

"Yes, absolutely. Thank you, Doctor."

"Alright then, I will see you next month for another check-up. Perhaps I will meet Thomas by then."

"Thank you, Dr. Jones," Amelia stated as she lowered herself off the hospital bed. Dr. Jones exited the room and I steadied Amelia as she gathered her things.

"Maybe you can eat something simple like a bowl of broth and rice. I can make it for you when we get back to my house."

"Okay. I need to lie down too. I'm so tired. I never thought I could feel like this. I gave my notice at the pool yesterday. There's only two weeks left of summer, but I'm just too tired to work. I think my mother is starting to worry. I have to tell her soon. I can't hide this for long."

Amelia and I walked out of the hospital and made our way into the parking lot. I looked at her while she spoke. I felt so sorry for her. This was a big deal. This was going to change her life forever. I knew that I was going to love this little baby. I knew that I was going to be the best auntie, but it was still going to be a struggle.

I was secretly nervous for her to tell my brother, as well. I knew she was stalling for the same reasons. I'm really not sure how he will react. He has always had this dream to play college baseball. Everything may be in jeopardy now. Everything would change.

I watched my friend as she gingerly got into the front seat of my car. She was so fragile. I couldn't stand to watch her like this.

"Come on Amelia, let's get you home."

Amelia placed her hand on my arm. "I don't know what I would do without you, Lucy. I love you so much. You truly are the best person in the world." She yawned.

I chuckled at her. "In the world? Wow...I must be really awesome." I looked over at Amelia. Her eyes were closed and I could tell she was already sleeping. I took a deep sigh.

Trouble...nothing but trouble.

CHAPTER 29

Lucy

Julia called while I was out. I guess she got my ten messages begging her to contact me. I settled Amelia in my bed, hoping she would get some rest while I started to make some dinner. I persuaded my father to put Mikey and the girls in camp for the last two weeks of summer. I convinced him that they were bored. He was feeling so much guilt that he reluctantly agreed. I thought that it was the best thing for them. There was only so much entertaining I could do. It also gave me some time to myself and to help Amelia with her current issues.

Camp kept these kids active and I knew by the time they came home, they would be starving. I decided to make a quick sauce so we could have pasta tonight. Mikey always liked pasta.

I picked up the phone and dialed Julia's number. I hoped she was home. It was so hard to reach her. The phone rang. No answer. I hung up.

"I'll never get a hold of her. We're both so busy," I said out loud to myself.

"What's that?" Julia asked as she came casually walking out of our dad's office, shutting the door behind her.

"*Julia!* What are you doing here? Where did you come from?" I asked, pleasantly amazed.

My sister laughed. "Surprised to see me?" Julia pulled up a chair at the counter.

"Yes, I was just calling you. I thought I was never going to reach you."

"Well, I got so many messages from you, I thought I'd better come home. You were starting to worry me. Besides, I have a little time off before next semester starts. I know you must be tired of looking after your brother and sisters."

"Actually, I convinced Dad to put the kids in summer camp. It's been a big relief."

"That's great! Although I'm surprised Dad was willing to pay for such an indulgence," Julia stated as she rolled her eyes at me. We didn't have a lot of money; at least that's what my father claimed.

"They'll be happy to see you, Julia. I think they're sick of me," I said, kidding. I walked around the counter and gave my sister a big hug. "I'm *so glad* to see you!" I said dramatically.

Julia laughed and shoved me away from her. "It's nice to be missed. So, what's so urgent? Why all the phone calls?"

I looked at Julia. I hadn't rehearsed how to bring up the subject of my mother without sounding weird. I'm not sure how much I could tell her, about the dreams and the visions. I turned and busied myself at the stove while I gathered my thoughts.

"I was thinking about Mama and her childhood. After she died, I realized I didn't know much about her life." Julia stared at me while I spoke. I had her attention. I definitely had her attention. "So, I went and spent an afternoon with Grandma. I thought she could maybe give me some insight. I went up into her old attic. Remember when we were young, how we use to play up there?" Julia smiled at the memory. "I went in the attic and rummaged through some old pictures. I found some of Great Grandma and some of the farm in Vermont. I found some old

183

pictures of Mom and her siblings. I also found an old picture of Great Grandpa, or I think it's him, having never actually met him."

"Grandma let you take the pictures? I find that hard to believe."

"Well, I grabbed a box and quickly put it in my car before she could object."

"Can I see the album?" Julia asked.

"Sure! I'll go get it." I ran up the stairs to my bedroom. I bent down and reached underneath my bed where the album was stored. I hadn't looked at the album since I went to my grandmother's that day, but something changed. The album looked old and battered, even though it was brand new. I tiptoed around Amelia, trying hard to be quiet. She was still fast asleep. I hope my supper doesn't turn her stomach. I carried the album downstairs to show Julia.

"Here it is, Julia." I placed the album on the counter in front of my sister. I stood behind her as she slowly turned the pages of the photo album. Julia knew more than me. She knew who was who and where many of the photos were taken.

"This one is of Mom when she was about four years old," Julia stated.

"Look how cute she was! Doesn't she look like Kaylan?" I asked.

Julia looked at me and nodded her head while she smiled. "I think we all look like her, in some way or another. So, what is it that you wanted to know about Mom?"

"You're going to think I'm crazy. Promise not to judge me."

Julia turned to me, concerned. "What is it?"

"I have these dreams. In them appears a creepy old man, with a doglike face. He's very dangerous. He tries to kill me."

Julia sat back, horrified by my nightmare. "That's awful!"

"It's okay, I've gotten used to them. I have this sense that Mama is trying to tell me something. I feel like something horrible happened to her when she was young. I can't explain it, it's just how I feel."

Julia looked at me with consideration. "This is between you and me, right? Do you understand?"

"Yes, I promise. I can keep a secret," I said.

"You said you have a picture of Great Grandpa in this album? Where is it?" Julia asked.

I turned through the pages of the book quickly, searching for the photo. All the plastic on the pages were torn and ripped, some photos lopsided and falling out of their slot.

"I don't know what happened to this album. It was in perfect condition when I placed the pictures in it," I said, confused. The picture of my grandfather was gone. In it's place, an empty slot. "This is so strange! I swear it was here, right where I placed it."

"Maybe Mikey got into it," Julia suggested.

"Maybe..." I said. I wasn't sure how that could be. Mikey didn't usually get into my personal things.

"It doesn't matter. I thought Mom had gotten rid of all those old pictures of Great Grandpa anyway. I'm surprised one still exists."

"Why would she destroy the pictures?" I asked, pulling up a chair next to my sister.

"I can only tell you what I've heard and witnessed. I don't know all the facts." Julia took a deep breath before she began. "It all happened one night at Grandma's house, a few years back. You weren't there; it was just Mom and me."

I nodded my head, encouraging her to continue.

"Mom had been drinking a little. Her and Grandma were having a heated discussion about Great Grandma's farm and whether they should sell it or not. Great Grandma had just died and Grandma was upset with her siblings. They had been fighting over Great Grandma's estate, the money, the farm, and all her furniture."

"I vaguely remember Mom telling Dad what a disgrace some of her family is. I always wondered what she was talking about," I added.

"Yes, well...it gets worse. Mom and Grandma started fighting and arguing. Mom was screaming at her, saying things like, 'You knew all along, how could you let him do that to me? Your father, he was a SICK BASTARD! He made me do things to him, things no child should ever experience.'

"I remember staring at Mom in shock as it started to register what it was she was saying," Julia went on.

187

"Mom was sexually abused?" I asked as I placed my hands over my ears. It was starting to make sense, but I couldn't bear to listen to Julia's words. All these years, trying to understand the forced relationship between my mother and my grandmother.

"Grandma's father, the man in the picture, he was an evil man," Julia said.

My mouth was slightly opened, dry and tasteless as I tried to comprehend the repulsive information my sister was sharing with me. "What did Grandma say?" I asked. "She couldn't have known; who would do that to their own child?"

"Grandma? Your sweet grandmother who tried to move in here a few months ago? The one Dad told to go to hell?"

I nodded, amazed at Julia's contempt for my grandmother.

"Well, she grabbed a fistful of Mom's hair and yanked her to the ground. She punched and kicked at her while she continued to berate her, telling her that she was a liar, an awful, awful liar."

"Oh my god!" I said as I stood, my hand over my mouth. "That can't be." I understood now, I totally understood but I couldn't share this with Julia. It was all too confusing.

"It's true. I was there and saw it with my own eyes."

I took a deep breath and thought about my mother, my poor mother, my little Sarah.

"Does Dad know?" I asked.

"Yes, we told him. He knows everything. He can't stand Grandma."

I heard Amelia making her way down the staircase.

"Where did you come from?" Julia asked, surprised to see Amelia.

I started to laugh and turned to Julia. "People just appear out of nowhere around here," I joked.

"Who else is in this house that I should know about?"

"Dead or alive?"

Julia rolled her eyes at me. "Hopefully living!"

"What on earth are you people talking about?" Amelia asked sleepily, confused.

"Never mind, Amelia. It's one of those things, you had to be there," I said. "Sit down here, I'll make you guys some tea." I gave Amelia my stool and turned to my sister.

"Thank you, Julia. You've been very insightful."

Julia glanced at me. "Glad I can help."

CHAPTER 30

Sam

Sam watched as Charles and Jimmy exited Kat's apartment, looking like they were in a big hurry to get somewhere real important. Did they all live together? Sam couldn't understand Kat. Who were these people? The tall skinny one, he would come and go at night, mostly alone, always in a hurry. Tonight, she was going to follow him to see where he went. Perhaps she would learn something about him. Maybe he could give her some insight into Kat's new single life.

Sam's apartment was riddled with mice and cockroaches. She tiptoed around the kitchen slowly, avoiding the sudden movement of a rodent that startled her every time. Her place was disgusting. She could hardly believe that she was staying here. She tried carefully not to touch anything; she wore gloves and body protection out of pure safety precautions, in spite of the blistering heat of the August sun. She hoped Kat appreciated what she did for her. She hoped she understood the sacrifices she made on her behalf.

She pulled out her automatic pistol and placed it on the table for cleaning. She removed the safety pin and unloaded the gun. She gingerly shined the metal casing until the reflection hurt her eyes. This was all the protection she needed. She couldn't live in a place like this, surrounded by convicts and drug addicts without some sort of protection. Her life was in danger here, and so was Kat's. Sam needed to protect her; Kat didn't know what she was doing.

Sam's basement apartment was lower than ground level, so when she looked out of her kitchen window, she could hear the voices of people and see their legs, but she could not see their faces. She oftentimes covered herself like a bum and sat out on the stoop of the apartment building. Kat's building was right next door so she could see her coming and going, never alone, always with that man. She supposed Kat was nervous to be alone now, after she experienced the confrontation with that street person, the day Demetry saved her life. She was oh-so grateful. She's disgusting with these men.

It was raining outside her window, which she was grateful for because it made hiding behind an umbrella easier and she wouldn't have to overdress in the heat. She needed to get ready. She didn't want to miss the opportunity to follow the skinny one, and it was getting late. The two men had already entered Kat's apartment. She looked at herself in the mirror. She pulled her hair back in a tight bun and yanked a baseball cap over her head. She grabbed a dark pair of sunglasses and put them on her face. She wore a light summer dress along with a raincoat and grabbed her umbrella. She quickly placed the small revolver inside her backpack and went outside to sit in the rain and wait.

She didn't have to wait long. The tall, skinny one was leaving the apartment under a hooded, oversized raincoat. She paced quickly behind him and followed him down the street. There were always people on the sidewalk. Several large brick apartment buildings lined both sides of the narrow street with an occasional privately owned storefront breaking up the monotonous stoops. Sam weaved in and out of the crowd and hoped that he didn't notice she was following him. He was headed toward the T, Boston's subway system. He jumped on eagerly to get out of the rain, and so did Sam with three others. She sat quietly in the last seat, several spots behind him. He spoke to the person in the next aisle. She could hear him joking about the weather and how hot it has been. He seemed very friendly.

She thought she recognized him. He was from their town, younger than she. He went to her high school. She hoped he didn't remember her.

The train rumbled and shook as they headed downtown, the lights flickering on and off. Several of the standing passengers quickly looked around to find steadier seating to avoid the abrupt movements of the jerky train. She could see flashes of lightening in the skyline as the rain splashed on the metal roof of the subway.

The train slowed down to its first stop and they got off. He quickly ran down the sidewalk half a block, covering his head from the deluge of rain and then ducked into a local pub. Sam followed him hurriedly and walked into the bar shortly after him. Protected by her umbrella, she watched him as he took a seat near the bartender, then she quickly slipped into the ladies room to fix herself. She removed her hat and let her curls down out of the tight bun. She shook her hair with her hands to remove any excess water and gave herself a good fluff. She removed her raincoat and placed the wet umbrella and coat back into her backpack. She fixed herself so that she looked presentable, adjusting and straightening her dress. She applied her glossy lipstick and pinched her cheeks. She didn't think he would recognize her.

She walked slowly back into the bar and took a seat a few chairs down from him and ordered a beer. The bartender was friendly and asked her what her name was.

"Annie," she said kindly. She always wanted to be an Annie. Ever since she was young and saw that little redheaded orphan girl play her character.

The bar seemed empty, just a few gentlemen watching the game on the television. Not too many people out on a stormy night, she guessed. She glanced over at the man…Jimmy was his name. That's right! She remembered now. She definitely went to school with him. A flush of nerves went through her chest and up her face. Perhaps he would recognize her, if she recognized him. She hoped not. She didn't want Kat to know she was here, in town, not yet anyway.

Jimmy appeared to be getting drunk, as Sam watched him consume a considerable amount of alcohol in only a very short period of time. She glanced over at him and he looked at her, oddly. She smiled as friendly and inviting as she possibly could. She glanced back at the bartender, who was also watching her intently. She hesitated, thinking this might be a bad idea. She should leave and go back home. She considered this option, but the rejection was too deep, too raw. How dare Kat do this to her? Sam would never understand. They loved each other. If Kat would just listen to her, they would have a great life together, they could be happy.

"Hello, sweetheart," Jimmy said, leaning over his chair toward hers.

"Hey, how are you?" she responded. *Stay friendly. Don't be rude.*

"Do you mind if I sit?" He stood and introduced himself. His words were slurred and his breath smelled like smoke. "My name is Jimmy. What's your name?"

"Annie."

"Annie, such a pretty name for a pretty lady."

She giggled a girlish laugh. She was disgusted with her behavior, but she needed to pretend. She needed to be nice. This man repulsed her, in his baggy jeans and stained, unkempt T-shirt. The bartender looked confused over her decision to be giving Jimmy any kind of attention. She smiled and put her hand up to his, to ease his worry that she was not being bothered.

"Can I buy you another drink?" Jimmy asked.

"Sure, that sounds nice. What a terrible night to be out, don't you think?" she asked, trying to continue the conversation.

"It is, especially for a woman." Jimmy stared at her for a moment. "You look so familiar," he said.

"I get that all the time. I must look like someone famous," she said, trying to change the subject.

"Yeah, that's it. A movie star, what's her name?" Jimmy swigged down his mug of beer to make room for the next.

"Oh, I don't know. I can't remember." Sam fluttered her eyelashes at Jimmy. She purposely dropped her apartment keys between the chairs and bent over to pick them up, granting Jimmy a good glance into her cleavage.

"Let me get that for you," Jimmy stated as he stood. He wobbled as he tried to move the chairs out of his way to help her.

"I've got it! Thank you," she said, appreciating his effort. *Don't fall over, you fool. You might get hurt!* This was so easy. "So, what do you do for work?"

"Me and my buddy, we run a fishing boat out of the harbor. We fish for tuna." Jimmy steadied himself as he sat back down in the chair closest to her. He had no shame in the way he allowed his eyes to settle on her thighs and how he eagerly stared at her breasts. He barely looked at her face when he spoke.

197

"Wow, that must be hard work. You must be a very strong man." Sam lightly placed her hand on his arm, effectively flirting with Jimmy as he sat across from her. Jimmy grabbed her hand and kissed the back of it disgustingly as he stared once again at her breasts.

"I can show you the boat, if you're interested. It's not far from here."

Sam considered his invitation. She'd like to see this boat. This must be where Kat spent all her time. What harm could it do?

"Yeah, why not? So this buddy of yours, you live together?" Sam asked as they stood and paid the bartender for their drinks.

"Yup. Unfortunately, his girlfriend lives with us too, so it's a little crowded. I come to the bar often just to get away from them. They're all lovey dovey, constantly touching each other. It's really uncomfortable for me. Of course, on nights like these and when I can meet someone as fine as you, then I'm a little grateful." Jimmy winked at Sam as he looked up and down her dress. She laughed her girlish fake laugh while she took out her raincoat and umbrella. She turned her back to Jimmy so he couldn't see the disgust in her face.

She couldn't believe Kat was in a relationship with a man. Her stomach soured at the thought of the idea. She could feel her color turn a bright red from the heat of her skin, while Jimmy continued to describe their seemingly affectionate relationship. She forced herself not to give up. She forced herself not to puke right here on the floor of the bar. It was far more than she could handle.

"That sounds really tough for you," she said to Jimmy while patting him on his back as they walked out onto the streets of Boston. The rain had let up slightly as they slowly started a jog toward the marina. She allowed Jimmy to hold her hand and lead the way, only out of sheer convenience. She didn't know where she was and she didn't want to confuse herself. She keenly looked around at the landscape and the businesses surrounding the bar so she could find her way back to the T when the time was right. The marina was close and she thought she could manage.

Jimmy stopped under a storefront canopy and dug into his pockets for a cigarette. Sam rolled her eyes as she watched him swagger to light the soggy cigarette, drenched from the rain. He got irritated and threw it to the ground.

"What do I need that for when I've got you here to satisfy me?" Jimmy growled under his nasty breath as he tried to wrap his arms around her waist. He eagerly kissed her neck and she quickly pulled herself away from him.

"Not here, Jimmy. Save it for the boat," she said convincingly. Jimmy looked at her, unsure, and then he grabbed her hand again and they made their way through the marina. It was dark and late and Sam looked around to see if anyone was out and about. The boats looked unsettled as the waves from the ocean storm rattled them back and forth against the docks. They climbed a set of metal stairs toward a few of the larger fishing vessels. Jimmy hopped up on one of them and grabbed her hand to pull her into the boat. The waves were vicious as they slapped against the sides of the vessel, making standing difficult, if not impossible. Jimmy yelled, "Follow me!" as he pulled her underneath the bow and into the small space located beneath the boat's deck.

The rain had grown increasingly heavier and louder as Sam shook herself off in the small room. The tiny kitchen area held a small coffee pot and refrigerator. The room also contained a small table that looked like it could convert into a bed, if need be. *We won't be needing that,* she thought to herself. Jimmy disappeared into the small bathroom to grab a towel as Sam quickly started to open the kitchen cabinets, searching the room for evidence. What she was looking for, she had no idea. She just needed to see. She needed to see how Kat lived here, with these men.

Jimmy entered the room again, drying his hair with a towel. "What are you doing?"

"Looking for beer," she answered quickly with a questioning smile.

Jimmy appeared to accept this answer willingly and kicked open the refrigerator, revealing a stash of alcohol.

"Help yourself," he said as he plopped down at the table, cracking open a beer for himself. "There's a few girly drinks in there that belong to Kat, but I'm sure she wouldn't mind if you drank one."

Just the mention of Kat's name made Sam's blood boil. The realization that Jimmy lived with her and spent time with her ignited a sense of rage and jealousy within her. She could feel the expression on her face change as he talked about her. She tried to remain calm and undetected.

Jimmy kicked a chair over in her direction and asked her to sit down. The simple fact that he kicked the chair at her made her want to punch him in his ugly face, let alone sit down with this man and have a drink.

She sat.

"Why don't you tell me a little about this Kat?" she asked casually. Jimmy's face also changed. She could tell instantly that he had feelings for her. This didn't surprise her. Kat ruined everyone's lives. Those who got close enough to her were eventually disappointed by the end results. She was a user. She did what was convenient for her, not for others. Jimmy shook his head and put his hands over his face.

"Well, that Kat…she's a special girl. We've been friends a long time." Jimmy threw his empty beer can aggressively into the garbage and grabbed another one. "I just don't understand Charles," he said miserably.

"Charles?" Sam asked with concern.

"Yeah, Kat's boyfriend. He can be a real asshole," Jimmy said as he swigged down another beer.

"Why's that?" she asked, completely interested.

"He's jealous of Kat and my's relationship. See, Kat gets really flirty and Charles can't handle that. I can't help it if she finds me attractive, but Charles gets angry. He won't let Kat anywhere near me now, not unless he's with her. He's really controlling. I can't wait to get away from them." Jimmy started to glare at Sam, like he's just realized that she was there, in the room with him. He threw another empty beer can in the trash.

Sam started to think about leaving. He was getting really drunk and she thought she had all the information she could get out of him.

"Get me another beer," he demanded as he stared across at her with a sour face. Sam recognized that look. The look of alcohol-induced anger. She stared back at him, thoughts of contempt running through her brain as she stood to get him another beer. She could hear the rain and see the lightning through the tiny portholes. The thunder cracked through the room, startling her as she bent down to take the beverage out of the refrigerator. Jimmy grabbed her waist and pulled her down onto his lap while the boat rocked her backpack off the counter and onto the floor.

A sense of fear rippled through her body as she realized how quick and strong Jimmy was, even in his state of drunkenness. He roughly held her hands in front of her chest with one hand, taking her completely off guard. She laughed nervously, trying desperately to get out of his clutches. He licked the back of her neck up and down as he held her still in place, unable to move.

"Hey, Jimmy? I think I need to head back now. I'm feeling a little seasick on this boat. Maybe we can go somewhere else. Somewhere more steady. I feel like I might get sick," she pled, her voice shaking with fear and uncertainty. What did she do? This was a big mistake.

Jimmy growled in her ear, "You'll be fine, little lady. Just be still and let Jimmy take care of you." Jimmy placed his free hand through the top of her damp, clingy sundress and cupped her breast. She laughed again, nervously.

"Please Jimmy, let me go. I don't feel good." She tried to pull her hands free from his grip, but his hands were large and he was relentless in his strength.

"You wanted this," he spat. "You asked me to bring you here." Jimmy pushed his leg through hers and spread them apart with his knee, leaving her completely vulnerable. She could feel his disgusting hard-on rubbing against her back as he continued to molest her body with his free hand. She tried to stand but he pulled harder on her hands, making her scream out in pain.

"You little bitch, this is what you're here for. Keep still or you'll be sorry." He seethed his words at her while he squeezed her wrists tighter together. She could feel the blood circulation restricted from her hands. She started to cry. She couldn't believe this was happening and how foolish she was to underestimate him. She wasn't thinking clearly. Her eyes went straight for her backpack. *My gun!* If she could get to her gun, she could scare him. What if he took it from her? What if he used it against her? Her mind was racing and she knew she was running out of time. Jimmy was moaning and making horrible, awful noises of pleasure.

Pretend. Pretend.

"Jimmy," she whispered as she threw her head back, giving him access to her chest. Her heart was racing with fear and rage. "Use both hands," she urged as she stopped resisting him. She moaned lightly to indicate the pleasure and passion she was pretending to feel. She spread her legs wider as she continued to sit on his lap, non-verbally consenting to the situation.

"Now, that's better," Jimmy said in her ear with his hot and nasty beer breath. He continued to rub her thighs and eagerly placed his hand inside her panties. His eyes closed as he busied his hands with her body. Men were so easily fooled. She waited for him to relax his grip and she quickly stood out of his reach and ran for her backpack.

Briefly surprised by her sudden escape, Jimmy leaped from the chair and grabbed the back of her hair and pulled her down to the ground. They fell hard together, the lightning and thunder surrounding them, her screams lost in the violent sounds of the storm. Sam scrambled across the floor and grabbed her bag, reaching in for the gun. She rolled over quickly to face Jimmy. He grabbed her throat with both his hands and started to squeeze the life out of her body.

Her eyes were wide with fear, her thoughts racing. He was going to kill her, he was going to kill her. She shoved the gun into Jimmy's chest and she pulled the trigger.

It all happened so fast. Jimmy's eyes stared into hers, the cloud of death hazing over them as he realized what just happened. His hand reached for his chest. He revealed the blood spilling over his pale, white fingers. Before he could speak, he collapsed on top of her shaking body.

Fear and panic struck her soul as she struggled to get him off of her. Sam pushed hard and turned him over on his back, the wound on his chest becoming more obvious.

"Jimmy…Jimmy!" She was instantly regretful. She didn't have a choice, she told herself. She stood in shock and looked carefully over the dead body. She looked down at her dress and noticed the blood-drenched stained garment. *Oh my god!* What did she do? She was so confused. She ran into the bathroom and looked into the mirror. She took a towel and rubbed the splattered blood off her face. Should she call the police? It was self-defense. What would Kat say? *She might implicate me.* This was all her fault!

Sam grabbed the gun and shoved it back into her bag. She reached for her raincoat and threw it on over her body. Gratefully, she realized it covered her bloody dress. She quickly scanned the cabin of the boat for any more evidence. She grabbed her drink and shoved it into her backpack. There was nothing else. *Fingerprints!* She wiped down the cabinets, table, and chairs where they sat.

She threw the bloodied towel into her bag and got ready to leave. She took her umbrella and walked back up the stairs onto the deck of the boat. She looked around the marina. She saw no one. She quickly ran down the metal stairs and back up the street toward the T. Her heart was racing with fear, her mind mangled by thoughts and explanations.

This was all Kat's fault. It was all her fault!

CHAPTER 31

Lucy

I decided to go to Anna's alone this time. I wanted to tell her about the information I discovered, about my mother and the abuse. I needed to talk about Jack. I was hoping she would have some more input. Maybe she would have suggestions on how to tell Thomas about the baby. Amelia and I planned to go visit him this weekend. I needed to get away and clear my mind. I needed to be supportive of Amelia; she was so sensitive right now. I hoped my brother would react positively. I didn't want to be around Amelia should he decide to act like a jerk. God only knows what she would do. I hoped for the best.

It was a beautiful drive over to Anna's. The trees were swaying in the warm summer breeze. The flowers were in full bloom, the air heavy with lilac. I thought of Jack and my heart ached as I recalled our last moments together. The words of his letter an unbelievable reminder of how foolish my trusting and vulnerable heart was. I dreamt about going to him, jumping into my mother's old car and driving the distance. I imagined arriving at the farm and finding him in the barn with his new girlfriend. The rejection and humiliation would be far too much for me to bear. I could never risk it. He wanted to move on; I should let him move on. It sounded logical enough, but my heart spoke differently. I was pretty sure that I would suffer like this forever and that I would never forget him. His decision was hurtful, but the disappointment of his actions even more devastating. I believed in him as a person, but now I questioned, what kind of person was he anyway?

I pulled into the long and winding driveway of the estate. It was even prettier than the first time I visited. I quickly made my way to the enormous front door and watched the housekeeper open it, even before I could knock.

"Hello, Miss Lucy. Anna is waiting for you in the gardens. I believe you can find your way."

"Yes, thank you, ma'am." I walked down the noisy hallway and through the double French doors out onto the patio. Anna was cutting long stem roses and placing them in her flower basket. The casual scene seemed so classic, like a picture cut out of a décor magazine. She was wearing her straw garden hat and delicate white gloves. Her casual sundress flirted with the breeze as she seemingly floated through her garden cutting flowers. She seemed so peaceful. You could sense that all this agreed with her, it kept her happy.

"Hello, Anna," I said like a small child.

"Lucy, sweetheart, I'm so happy you came." Anna approached me with her hands stretched out, eager to take mine. She walked me through her garden, her arm around mine. She was far more affectionate than last visit and I instantly felt welcomed in her home.

"How have you been? How's Amelia feeling?" she asked.

I looked at her, confused at her questioning, but decided to assume that she knew about the baby.

"We've been busy, to say the least," I responded.

"Everything will be alright, with Amelia. She'll be fine."

I knew that she was right. I shouldn't worry. Amelia was one of the strongest persons I knew, with or without my brother. She would manage just fine.

"Jack?" she asked.

I took a deep breath that felt like one hundred pounds as I let it escape my body, leaving room for the emotions that I had been desperately trying to avoid. Anna stopped and looked down into my face. She was like an older, sweeter version of Julia, warm and considerate, attentive to my needs, as a mother would be to her child. I could feel my mouth start to quiver as I tried to smile at Anna, to reassure her that I was okay. "Jack, he's gone now. He doesn't want me." I suddenly felt the urge to throw my arms around Anna and cry into her pretty sundress, willing her to soothe away my sadness and heartache. Hoping she could make it better for me. Anna wrapped her arms around my waist and held me while I cried.

She whispered sweet words of comfort. "You're a strong girl, Lucy; I promise you'll get through this."

I gathered myself carefully while Anna handed me some tissue she had in her pocket.

"Do you feel better?" she asked.

I did. It was hard to be strong; it was hard to care for everyone, shoving hurt and mournful feelings aside while you moved on in your day. I was desperate for support and understanding, for someone to take interest, for someone to listen to me. I wanted to feel sorry for myself, just for a moment or two.

"Thank you, Anna. I'm sorry for that, it's just been so difficult. I don't know who to trust anymore."

Anna looked at me. "You go through life and you trust people, you stay honest with yourself. You need to continue to be vulnerable at times. It's a part of life, the pain we feel, the pleasure we feel, and the confusion. It's how we learn."

I nodded as she spoke, her words important to me, her advice valuable.

Anna and I walked past the small sunroom and over to the gazebo at the far end of the garden. It was lovely, absolutely lovely. The gardens were even more spectacular than last time I visited.

"It's a breathtaking garden, Anna. You've really outdone yourself," I stated in awe at her ability.

"It takes years, Lucy, but I enjoy what I do. When you have a passion in life, you will find that those things you feel passion for will flourish."

I glanced at Anna, doubtful that I could ever be as successful at gardening as she.

"You're young, Lucy; you have a lifetime yet to figure out what your passions are. You will, I have no doubt."

It's like she reads my thoughts.

Anna glanced over her gardens and smiled pleasantly. We continued to stroll through the walkways and sat down on the bench underneath the gazebo. The sounds of the large water fountains sprinkling rainwater pleasantly resonated in our ears.

Anna's housekeeper appeared with refreshing lemonade and sugar cookies. I could live here. I felt so relaxed, so at ease. "Thank you, Agnes," I said as I reached for the glass. No one waited on me at home. This was heaven.

Anna and I sat back and peacefully shared a quiet moment. It was relaxing and serene and I didn't want it to end. Anna glanced at me for several moments, and a look of understanding appeared on her face.

"You seem different, Lucy. More confident?" she asked.

I laughed. I guess you could say that. "I feel more comfortable with my newfound abilities," I responded. "I'm not afraid anymore."

Anna nodded her head understandingly. "Your mother, she's here."

"Yes, I sense her. She's sitting on the bench next to the roses. She loves your garden," I said gratefully.

Anna smiled. "I appreciate that." Anna paused, then asked, "Who's Sam?"

I stared at her, unsure of who she was talking about.

"I'm not sure," I responded.

Anna looked concerned and confused. "Again, your sister Kathryn dominates my thoughts. I feel uneasy."

A quick ripple of fear entered my chest as I thought about Kathryn. I didn't want to acknowledge my dream or the implications. I didn't want to speak the words or ask the questions. I couldn't risk it.

"Well, it may come up again, sometime in the future," Anna replied. "Things with your mother, she seems more settled, peaceful?"

"Yes, I think so. You were right about her childhood. She was abused by her grandfather." Speaking the words felt surreal as I thought about my poor little Sarah. She was so sweet and innocent. The pain and suffering she endured was heartbreaking.

"She's glad, you know. She wanted you to know. She felt that she had to explain why she became so disconnected. It's brought her closure," Anna explained.

"It does explain a lot. I still feel so guilty. I wish I could have helped her. I wish she were here with us, taking care of us. I miss her terribly," I said, a knot of pressure lodged in the back of my throat as I tried to force back the pain.

"She's very proud of you," Anna said. "She's grateful. She wants you to know that she chose to give up. There was nothing you could have done to prevent it."

"Thank you, Anna. I appreciate that."

"Are you taking a trip?" Anna asked, surprised.

"Yes, I think so. I think we'll go visit my brother up in Boston this weekend. My sister Julia is in town for the next two weeks, so it's now or never."

"Be careful, Lucy. I feel a huge amount of anxiety over this trip."

She sensed my fear of confronting Thomas about the baby. I had anxiety as well, for Amelia. It was time he knew. We couldn't keep this from him forever.

"I will. I'll be extra cautious."

I laughed at those words weeks later. Cautious, I was never.

CHAPTER 32

Sam

Sam stood in her kitchen, drenched from the rain, unable to move her legs. Her thoughts were confused and scattered. Did she just kill Jimmy? The fear and realization paralyzed her brain. What did she do? Charles would most likely discover his body within the hour, when he goes to work. He would wonder why Jimmy didn't come home last night, but perhaps that wasn't unusual.

She didn't have much time. The police would be called. No one knew who she was, no one saw her but the bartender. He could identify her, but he didn't know her real name.

She took a deep breath and looked over herself. Feelings of anger began to spread through her body as she hurriedly removed her raincoat. She ripped the blood-soaked sundress from her body and shoved it in a plastic bag. She dragged herself into the bathroom and jumped into the moldy shower. She needed to get it off her, all that blood. She grabbed a washcloth and scrubbed her body clean, head to toe. She allowed herself several moments to feel the warmth of the water hitting her face. She cleared her thoughts and made a plan. She didn't have much time. She needed to hurry.

She quickly got dressed and packed her meager bag of clothing and subtle toiletries. She looked throughout the apartment. She had nothing personal there. Everything she owned fit into her backpack. She took her gun and wiped it clean, then reloaded the gun and checked the safety.

It was 5:00 in the morning. Charles would be leaving soon. She stood by her window and waited for him to pass her apartment. Although she couldn't see his face, she knew when he passed. She had watched him everyday and he was unmistakable. His boots were heavy and loud, his body lean and strong. Not many people passed at this time, making identifying him easier, and she was thankful for that.

She stood near the window, straining her neck when she heard the sound of Charles' boots trudging down the sidewalk. She quickly slipped outside her apartment door and watched him from the stoop to make sure it was him. She watched him

218

disappear around the corner and then she ran down the stairs and up Kat's stoop to ring the bell. She hoped that Kat would think that she was Charles and that he had forgotten something.

Sam rang the buzzer and just as she suspected, Kat responded and unlocked the door for her. Sam quickly made her way up the stairs toward her apartment. She knocked quietly, standing away from the peephole, just in case Kat glanced out. Sam could hear her from behind the door, fumbling with the locks. Her heart was pounding rapidly as she waited for Kat to open the door.

"Did you forget something?" Kat asked as she cracked the door open.

Sam shoved her foot between the door and the hallway. She pushed the door open, knocking Kat out of the way and into her kitchen table.

"What the hell! What the hell are you doing here!?" Kat yelled.

Sam had the gun to her side, the safety locked because she could never imagine killing Kat or living here on Earth without her. She needed it so Kat would listen to her, she didn't want to fight. She needed Kat to cooperate, to do what she said.

"Sit down and shut up." Sam pointed the gun at Kat's chest. Kat's eyes were wide with surprise. Sam could see the sudden fear spread across her face as her reality began to sink in. She looked beautiful when she was scared. Her short T-shirt, her tanned legs exposed, her breasts free from restraints beneath her shirt, she was so vulnerable. Sam had dreamt of this moment, the moment when they could be alone together again. It was all she had thought about.

"You and I, we have a problem, Kat."

CHAPTER 33

Lucy

Getting out of town with Amelia felt like the right thing. I felt temporarily freed from my emotions, excited to do something different for a change. We drove up the interstate with the music playing, the windows opened and eager to see Boston, a first trip of many to come. My brother called the house ten times this morning, wondering if we'd left yet. I could tell he was anxious to see Amelia.

I looked over at my best friend and she was smiling, happy and relieved to be feeling better, finally. Her symptoms were subsiding and she seemed relatively calm to be facing my brother. I'm sure the stress and the anticipation of telling him has weighed on her mind the last month. It was soon to be over.

I left Kathryn a message that we'd be coming to her apartment first. I didn't get to speak with her but I had her address. She was going to be so surprised to see us. I knew she had been feeling homesick.

The traffic into the city picked up and our travel slowed. I could feel my knuckles gripping the steering wheel as I made my way through the cars. The palms of my hands were sweaty with apprehension. I should have practiced driving more. I didn't know how to drive in a city. I looked over at Amelia once again, hoping for some encouragement.

"What's wrong, Lucy?" she asked with a grin on her face.

"Look! Look at my hands!" I stated frantically.

"Oh, stop it. You're doing fine. It's just a little traffic. Do you want me to drive?"

I sat up as straight as I could and looked ahead at the traffic. "Um, no. I don't think you're in any position to drive. What if you get sick all of a sudden and a big tractor-trailer truck is on your ass? You're all emotional; you'll probably swear at him and give him the finger. Then he may decide to run us off the road. Then what?" I looked at Amelia, whose eyes were wide open as I described the scenario of her driving.

"Well, that's a bit dramatic, don't you think?"

I started to laugh at her nonchalant attitude. She knew damn well that she was a bad driver. Way worse than me.

"Just pay attention for me. Watch the signs for Fenway Park. That's our exit."

Amelia sat up in her seat and took out the map and our directions. She was a perfect co-pilot. We were definitely going to get lost and we were both going to blame my brother for it. He should have picked us up, after all.

I navigated off the highway and after a few wrong turns we eventually located my sister's neighborhood. As I drove down the one-way street, I was a little surprised by the location of her apartment. I envisioned a little more glamor for Kathryn. This was definitely the opposite of glamor. Completely run down and scary, to be honest. No wonder Anna had so much anxiety. This was no place for my sister. I wasn't even sure that I wanted to stop my car. I had to think about Amelia.

"Are you sure this is where Kat lives, Lucy?" Amelia asked, seemingly concerned for our safety and welfare.

"Um, this is what the address says. I don't think we should stop. I think we should go find Tommy." There was no way I was stopping.

"Wait! There's Tommy! Right there!" Amelia yelled suddenly. I looked ahead down the street and she was right. Tommy was there, talking with a police officer. I suddenly felt completely at ease because Thomas was near, but then why was Tommy here anyway? I pulled over in the first spot I could find and Amelia jumped out of the car. She made her way down the sidewalk, ignoring the looks and inappropriate whistles as she clambered closer to Tommy. He suddenly saw her and quickly stepped to embrace her. I locked the car doors and followed suit down the same sidewalk. I was shocked at the stupidity of men with their dumb comments and looks as I made my way toward Tommy.

My brother's look on his face worried me. He was not as happy as he should be. I tried to calm my nerves as I approached the police officer. I closed my eyes and said a quick prayer. All the warnings and dreams of Kathryn drifted around in my head. I wanted to see Kathryn come running out of her apartment, amazed and happy to see us.

"Hey Tommy. Surprised to see you here, what's going on? Where's Kat?" I knew something was wrong. I was frightfully scared at what I was about to hear.

"Come inside to the apartment. I'll explain once we are off the street," Tommy said.

We followed him up the stairs and into the apartment. Tommy held Amelia's hand and glanced over at me with worry in his eyes. My heart sank. *Please, God. Please.*

We walked into the meager apartment and I noticed an officer sitting at my sister's kitchen table.

"Detective Nicholas, this is my sister Lucy and my girlfriend Amelia." Tommy introduced us to the detective as he stood and approached me and shook my hand. I watched him as he moved. His white casual dress shirt was rolled over his strong arms, revealing traces of tattoos and strength underneath it. His dark hair was short and tight and his eyes, dark and serious. Young and handsome, I questioned how he could be a detective; he looked only slightly older than I.

"Nice to meet you ladies," he said dryly. I watched the detective shake Amelia's hand and then he leaned against the counter, taking out his pencil and pad.

"Do you mind if I ask you girls a few questions?" Detective Nicholas looked directly at me, his eyes penetrating and unmistakably concerned.

"I want to know what's going on. Where's my sister? Where's Kat, Thomas?" I looked at my brother. I could hear my voice quiver as I asked the questions.

"Lucy, please, take a seat." The detective motioned for me to sit in his vacated chair. I stayed where I was and waited for an answer. I could feel my emotions ripple through my chest as I waited for them to speak. The detective looked at my brother and nodded his head, urging him to address me.

"Kat's missing, Lucy. She's not here. We don't know where she is. There's been an incident…Jimmy's been murdered."

Amelia and I stared at each other, shocked at what my brother was saying. A knot appeared in the back of my throat as I tried to speak, unable to comprehend all that was happening.

"What do you mean she's missing? Where could she be? Where is Charles?" Crazy thoughts began to run through my head. Are they on the run? Are they responsible for this? Maybe they're in danger.

Detective Nicholas started to speak. His relaxed posture and mannerisms worried me. How much experience could he have? His eyes, they appeared to have maturity; he was intelligent and respectful when he spoke. I was so taken aback by him; he was alarmingly handsome and not what I would expect of a police detective.

"Lucy, when was the last time you spoke with your sister Kathryn?"

I thought back to last week, when Kathryn called to say she'd be coming home soon. She sounded so excited about her decision to visit. She told me how much she missed everyone.

"I spoke to her last week. I tried to call her yesterday and today, but I never got a hold of her. I left her a message on her phone."

"What time yesterday?" the detective asked. I looked over at Amelia. She was with me when we made the call.

"I think it was around 11:00 yesterday morning."

Amelia nodded her head to confirm. The detective wrote in his journal.

"What's being done about this? We need to find them. What if they're in some kind of danger?" Thomas stated aggressively.

The detective glanced up at Thomas. "Do you know anybody who would want to hurt your sister or Charles in any way? Does anyone come to mind?"

"Who would want to hurt them?" I asked.

"Perhaps anyone who lives on this street in this damn neighborhood!" Tommy stated angrily. The officer's line of interrogation was noticeably starting to annoy him.

Amelia suddenly grabbed hold of my arm and started to cry. "I don't feel good, Lucy. I'm going to be sick." Amelia covered her mouth and ran through the apartment to the bathroom and slammed the door. My brother looked at me confused by the abrupt interruption. I thought about poor Amelia. This was all she needed, a murder mystery.

"Listen Tommy, I think we should get Amelia out of here. Perhaps she could go with you, and I could follow the detective down to the police station to answer his questions."

I knew as soon as I said it, Tommy would reject my idea. He didn't realize how unhelpful he could be. His attitude was aggressive when things weren't going his way. He needed to take care of Amelia now. She needed to be in a better place, all of which I couldn't explain to him while we were sitting here with the detective.

"I think that's a great idea," the detective added. "Lucy can fill me in on all the information that I need."

Amelia walked out of the bathroom, her face pale and lifeless. "Are you okay?" I asked her.

"I need to lay down, Lucy."

I walked over and held her arm as she moved across the floor.

"Thomas, can you take her home?" I asked again.

"What is wrong with you, you're sick?" Thomas asked Amelia. Amelia's eyes welled with tears as she considered Thomas' question and his bad attitude toward her. I'm sure that she understood that it wasn't her that he was angry with, but she was still so sensitive.

"I'm so worried for Kathryn. This is all so confusing." Amelia sat and put her hand on her forehead. Her arms were shaking terribly and her lip quivered as she spoke.

"Really Tommy, this isn't good for her. She needs to lie down. I don't want her to pass out."

"Why would she pass out? She acts like she's the one missing. My sister is missing, dammit! Why don't *you* take her back home? I'll stay here and help the detective with the investigation." Tommy began to pace back and forth in the kitchen.

I looked up at Nicholas. His eyes were fixed on me, watching the conversation with interest. I glanced over at Amelia. She had her head down on the table, crying into her arms.

"You're such a jerk, Thomas." I walked over to Amelia and helped her to her feet. "We're leaving!" I said as angrily as I could.

Thomas stood back and looked at us as we started to leave the apartment.

"Wait, I'll help her," he said as he tried to grab on to her arm.

Amelia glared up at my brother. "You want to help me now?" Amelia stood tall and looked up at Thomas. "Guess what, Tommy? I'm pregnant! That's what's wrong with me."

Tommy looked at Amelia, shock registering on his face.

"I don't want your help now! Stay away from me."
Amelia continued toward the door.

Tommy finally jumped into action as he realized his
pregnant girlfriend was about to walk down one of the most
dangerous streets in Boston.

"Wait, wait, wait. I'll take you home. I'm sorry…how was
I supposed to know?" Tommy looked at me quickly. "You
okay?"

"Yes, I'll be fine. Isn't that right, Detective?" I glanced
over at Nicholas, eager for them to leave.

"Absolutely. I'll make sure she's safe and sound. We'll
call you soon. Thank you for your time," he stated.

Tommy and Amelia left the apartment, arguing as they
walked down the stairs. Amelia was giving Tommy hell for being
such a jerk and Tommy was apologizing continuously for his bad
behavior. *So much for a subtle surprise.*

I glanced back up at the detective as he stared at me. I
shook my head. "I apologize for that. Everything is a little
screwed up in my family."

"No, please, it's perfectly okay." An awkward silence
lingered as I considered my next question.

"Would you like to go to the station now?" Detective Nicholas asked.

"Absolutely."

CHAPTER 34

Jack

Angie snuggled into my arms as we lay in bed together. I could see a slow smile spread across her face as she held my fingers in between hers. Her naked thigh was draped over my leg, relaxed, content, and satisfied. I could hear the phone ringing in the kitchen, but I hesitated to stand and answer it. Pop and Susie Mae left early that morning to attend the country fair for three days. Perhaps it was them, letting me know they've arrived safely.

I dragged myself out of bed and grabbed a towel to cover myself. Angie moaned lightly, complaining as I left the room.

I walked down the stairs and into the kitchen to answer the phone. My heart sank into my stomach as I listened to the man on the other line. Angie appeared on the stairs behind me.

"What is it?" she asked, concerned.

I turned and looked at her.

"It's a detective from Boston. Charles has been arrested."

CHAPTER 35

Lucy

I sat in the hallway of the busy police station as I waited for Detective Nicholas to finish talking with his boss. I looked around the room and watched as several people in handcuffs were transported into the secured area behind the main desk of officers. The police station was large with big open windows looking down onto the streets of Boston. The room was filled with old mahogany woodwork and classic brick walls. The floors were wide boards with knots and holes. You could see clearly through them to the bottom of the next floor.

I sat nervously folding my hands back and forth and over one another. I tried to close my eyes, to get a sense of my sister. I was surrounded by too much noise and activity that it was virtually impossible. She would show up somewhere. She has got to. There was no way my family could handle another devastating tragedy.

I watched Detective Nicholas exit the room at the far end of the building. He hurriedly walked through the office cluttered with desks, clerks, and police officers. I stood as I watched him approach, hoping he had new information for me. Detective Nicholas punched in a key code that allowed me to enter into the secured area behind the reception desk. I walked through the door and quietly followed him into a small private office. He quickly shut the door behind us and it instantly got quiet.

Nicholas walked behind the desk and sat with his hands folded on the table. "Sorry you had to wait, Lucy. Can I get you a glass of water? Coffee maybe?"

"No, thank you. I'm fine. Did you find my sister?" I asked quickly, anxious for an answer. The only answer I wanted to hear was yes, of course.

"No, I'm sorry. We haven't." He pulled out his pencil and pad and flipped it over to the page of notes he had been working on. "So, you spoke with Kathryn last week? How did she seem, on the phone with you? Did she act nervous? Was there any sign or indication that something could have been wrong?"

I looked at the detective, guilt spreading through my chest as I thought about Kathryn. "When we spoke, she seemed relieved and happy to be coming home for a visit. I got the sense that she was homesick." I thought back to our conversation. I had been so distracted by Amelia's problems; I wasn't really paying attention to her. I wasn't sure if she was acting strangely. Maybe I was missing something. I looked back at the detective. "Her and Charles seemed very happy. In fact, I've never seen my sister so content and settled."

Nicholas nodded his head and wrote in his notebook. I watched him as he worked. He was a young detective but I sensed that he had a lifetime of experience. When he spoke to me, he held my attention. He asked smart questions; he was thorough and attentive.

"How do you feel about Charles? Do you know him well?" Nicholas asked.

I stared into his eyes, unsure of my answer. "We lived in the same neighborhood growing up, until Charles was about sixteen years old. Unfortunately, his mother died and he and his brother Jack were relocated. We ran into Charles again this past year and my sister and I reunited him with his brother and grandfather. I can't vouch for Charles; I honestly don't know him that well. When I think about him, however, I don't get the sense

237

that he's dangerous or capable of harming anyone. My sister and he are certainly not capable of *murder*." I could feel my voice waver a bit as I talked to Detective Nicholas. I was trying hard to remain strong and unemotional. I just wanted to see my sister. I wanted to know if Kat was okay.

"We've found Charles and we've placed him in custody for now."

"*What?*" I sat up straight in my chair and leaned over the desk that separated the two of us. "You found Charles? You arrested him? For what?" I asked, shocked and confused. "Where's Kat?"

"Well, that's the problem, Lucy. He's unable to tell us where Kat is." Nicholas stood, walked over to the cooler, and poured a glass of water. He handed the cup to me. I accepted the drink and began to notice in more detail the tattoos that ran up and down his forearms. One forearm had a tattoo of a cross, while the other had a tattoo of an eagle. Old looking tattoos with black and green ink. The kind of tattoos my grandfather had after he came home from the war.

I glanced up at Nicholas as he leaned against his desk in front of me. A sense of terror spread throughout my body as I thought about Kat and where she was, who she was with, what she was doing. Was she safe, was she scared? I could feel the overwhelming sense of helplessness as I fought back my tears. I tried to focus on the investigation.

"I thought she was with Charles. I thought perhaps they went away for the weekend or maybe they were fishing off another boat. I felt that at least if she was with Charles, that he would keep her safe." I shook my head back in forth in denial. Maybe my thinking was all wrong. Charles was here and he doesn't know where Kat is, or at least that was what he was saying. Could Charles be responsible for Jimmy's murder? This couldn't be.

I couldn't fight it any longer. My voice cracked while my eyes filled with tears. I covered my face and started to cry.

Nicholas knelt down in front of me and took my hand and covered it with his. "I promise, Lucy, I'm going to do everything I can to find her. I won't stop until I do."

I looked up at Nicholas. I looked into his handsome, young face. I could hear Anna's words in the back of my mind: "You have to trust people, Lucy." I decided to trust this man. For desperate reasons, I needed to believe the words that he said.

"Please, Nicholas. We have to save my sister."

CHAPTER 36

Kathryn

"What the hell are you doing here, Sam? Why are you pointing a gun at me?"

Kat looked at her ex-girlfriend; how did she ever love her? She felt like they were strangers, like Sam became someone she had never met before. Has she lost her mind? Kat sat down in the chair at her table and waited for Sam to explain herself. Sam looked disheveled and nervous. Her hands shook as she held the gun pointed at her chest.

"We've got a big problem, and it's all your fault!" Sam began to pace the kitchen floor as she talked wildly to Kat, blaming her for all of her life's mishaps.

"Jimmy's dead," she stated calmly and evenly, as if she just told Kat the weather forecast for the day. "Did you know he was in love with you? Did you catch that about him, or are you too stupid to realize the effect you have on people? You ruin people, Kat! That's what you do, and then they die!"

Did she just say Jimmy's dead? Kat's mind began to race as sudden fear began to creep into her veins. This girl was crazy. She killed Jimmy? Why?

"What do you mean, Jimmy's dead? What did you do, Sam?"

Sam glared at her; she appeared ready to attack Kat's words with her crazy philosophies on how Kat ruined everybody's lives.

"Whatever happened, I'm sure we could fix this. We need to call the police."

Kat felt a sudden sense of urgency, a sense that perhaps Jimmy wasn't dead, but seriously injured. She needed to call someone. She needed to convince her.

Sam pointed her gun at her as she spoke. Spit and phlegm escaped her mouth as her angry words seeped from her tongue. "I'm not going to jail, Kat. This wasn't my fault. If you had just given me time, we could have worked this all out. But you didn't. You wouldn't even speak to me. Now I'm here and Jimmy is dead. What was I supposed to do, go on living without you? I couldn't. It was impossible!"

A million thoughts went flying through Kat's head. She looked at the phone hanging on the wall. She thought about calling the police, but then she reconsidered. The police didn't hurry to this part of town. If Sam was capable of killing Jimmy, she could be capable of killing her. Charles! What about Charles?

"Sam, this seems crazy. Why are you doing this? Our breakup doesn't warrant you running around killing people and sticking a gun into my chest."

"It's because of that man, Charles, isn't it? He has turned you against me."

"He doesn't even know about you!" Kat knew as soon as she said the words that they were a big mistake.

Sam turned and looked at her with a world of hurt in her eyes. She looked confused, like she couldn't fathom this, a relationship with a man.

"You think you could just erase our relationship, as if it never happened? No one knows about me, not your family, not

242

your boyfriend. You've always been embarrassed. I think it's disgusting, how you live."

Sam didn't look well. Her face was pale and ashen, her hair was damp and disheveled as if she forgot to comb it when she got out of the shower. Her eye makeup was still dark and running beneath her eyes, as if she forgot to wash it clean. She looked like she'd lost it. Tears filled her eyes as she sat down on a chair and started to shake and cry.

Kat reached out to her one more time. She spoke gently, kindly to soothe her and to calm her. "Sam, we can figure this out. We need to get help to Jimmy. Let's start there. Where is he?"

"He's on your boat. Your lover should be discovering him at any moment."

Kat thought about Charles. Thank god he was safe. Kat stood from her chair and Sam quickly stood as well, pointing her gun back at her.

"Where are you going?" Sam asked.

Kat put her hands up into the air to reassure her that she meant her no harm. "Can I get dressed Sam, please."

"That's a great idea. We need to leave this place."

243

Kat turned around slowly and walked back into her bedroom to put some clothes on. Sam followed quickly behind her, the gun close to her back. Kat opened a drawer and pulled out some shorts and a simple top.

"Don't make any quick movements and keep your hands where I can see them." Sam casually leaned against Kat's bedroom wall. Kat looked over at her, annoyed and dismayed over her current situation. She wanted to kick her ass, but Sam had the gun.

"Turn around, Kat, and face me. I want to watch you dress," Sam said viciously. Her words created an instant gag reflex as bile climbed quickly from Kat's stomach and into her mouth. She needed to get away from her. She couldn't think quickly enough.

Kat swiftly removed her shirt and covered herself with her arms. She glanced briefly over into Sam's eyes, not wanting to encourage her or to give her any satisfaction. Kat knew she enjoyed this, humiliating her.

"Put your arms down," Sam said as she used her gun to move Kat's arm. Kat rolled her eyes and took a deep breath. She stood there, in her bedroom, dressed in only her panties, while Sam's eyes wandered all over her body, watching and glaring. She waited for her command. Sam was going to try to make love to her. She knew where this was going, she has been here before.

"Sam, if we don't leave soon, the police may come looking." Kat watched her face as she remembered now that she has murdered someone. Kat prayed it was enough to distract her. She watched Sam's eyes glance over at the clock on the wall.

"Get dressed!" she said quickly as she angrily walked back into my kitchen, completely agitated. Kat threw on her shorts and T-shirt and looked for her sneakers. She laced her shoes and walked back into the kitchen. She stood there waiting while Sam grabbed her backpack.

"Do you have any money?" Sam asked.

"No," Kat answered dryly.

Sam carefully put her weapon back into her backpack. "Don't get any funny ideas, Kat," she said as she shoved her through the front door.

"Where are you taking me?"

"Shut up and don't ask any questions."

Kat walked ahead of Sam as they made their way outside the apartment building and down the sidewalk. They walked quickly toward the T and got on. Sam sat close to Kat and held her arm tightly.

Kat looked around the T at all the strangers in front of them. She wasn't sure what was worse, Sam with a gun or the people on the train. She kept her mouth shut. Sam was unstable, but Kat wasn't convinced that she would harm her. At least, that was what she hoped.

CHAPTER 37

Detective Nicholas

Detective Nicholas sat at his desk looking over his notes, trying to decipher whether Kat's case was a stranger abduction, or if there was some kind of love quarrel going on. All fingers would seem to point at Charles, the boyfriend, but for some reason, Nicholas believed his story. It all seemed so odd, the chain of events leading up to Kat's disappearance.

Nick's caseload was heavy, an unfortunate side effect to becoming a lieutenant detective. His sergeant continued to push him and encouraged him to work hard, long hours, being the best that he could be. Nick understood he needed to put in his time; he wanted and welcomed the challenge. His social life suffered, however, leaving him with no time to do the things that he loved to do. He enjoyed spending time with his family; he needed to spend more time with his mother. He was always eager to help the younger, less fortunate kids in his old neighborhood find direction in their lives. He knew what it was to have a respected father figure. He knew what it did for his own life; it kept him out of trouble.

Alex walked through the door of Nicholas' office. Alex was Nick's partner, a good friend and companion. They worked hard, long hours together, sharing many meals, and Nick was grateful for their instant bond and friendship. Without Alex, he would have felt alone in his department, among the older men and more experienced detectives. Alex was young and energetic; he was passionate and fearless, always eager to run out and get the bad guys. Nicholas was a little more reserved, a little more responsible and democratic. They were a perfect team.

Nick looked up from his notes and smiled as his friend. Alex plopped himself down in his chair.

"What's up?" Nick asked.

"Still following up on a couple more leads regarding that son of a bitch, Anthony Massimo. Do you have time today to take a ride?"

"Can't do it. I have a murder to investigate and a missing persons case, all connected somehow, but can't seem to figure out how yet."

"Yeah, I noticed the girl yesterday. Her family's in trouble?"

"Yes." Nick stood from the desk and reached for the filing cabinet, pulling out a file.

"She's attractive."

"She is." Nicholas glanced over at his friend.

"I need you back on this case with me. It's important, far more important than a missing persons case. Hand it over to someone else, maybe that lazy fuck Mark. He can try to work harder; he's always sitting on his ass."

Detective Nick started to laugh. "This is true. I want to help her, though; there's something I like about her. I can handle this, it will be a quick investigation and I'll be back on our case in no time." Nick could hear Detective Alex take a deep sigh of defeat.

"Well, I hope she's worth it."

"She is," Nick said confidently.

CHAPTER 38

Lucy

I slept restlessly that night in my brother's dorm room. Horrible dreams and nightmares invaded my sleep as I dreamt of my mother. Thomas and I decided not to tell my father that Kathryn was missing. We decided to tell him when it became absolutely necessary. We both believed that she would show up soon. My dreams indicated differently, but I refused to acknowledge them. Nothing made sense.

I thought about calling Jack but I couldn't bring myself to do it. I picked up the phone several times and then hung it back on the hook. I'm sure Charles will notify him. I convinced myself that I didn't need to be involved in that process.

I persuaded Tommy to drive Amelia back to Connecticut to her mother's house. It was the best place for her. She didn't need to be involved in this matter and Thomas could be more helpful if she was back home, safe.

I took a quick shower and dressed. I wanted to join Detective Nicholas today as he questioned some of the people down at the marina. He encouraged me to assist him, saying that I may have some insight into certain things from our past, things that he may not be aware of. I asked him if I could carry a gun. His stern and purposeful look told me *No!* But then he smiled. I thought about the detective. He was a strong, powerful man with a gun. There was something I liked about him, but I couldn't quite put my finger on it.

I walked out of Thomas' dorm room and into the police car waiting to escort me to the station. I watched the police officer maneuver through the streets of Boston toward downtown. I observed the crowds of people as they filled the sidewalks, some of them residents, some of them students and vacationers. The buildings were beautiful and historic. Brick, old architecture, and beautifully detailed buildings, large double door entrances, inviting you in, adorned with character and history. Large churches and universities filled my sights as I thought about how wonderful visiting Boston would be when we weren't in the middle of a crisis. When things weren't so screwed up.

I thought about telling Nicholas about the visions and the dreams. Maybe he would understand them or have some insight as to their meaning. I wished Anna were here. I tried to call her, but she was out of town. She could have helped me, I was sure.

I sat quietly in the back of the police car as it pulled up to the bar, not far from the marina. I looked around puzzled, but then relaxed when I saw Detective Nicholas walking through the bar doors. I thanked the driver and exited the vehicle. Nicholas greeted me on the sidewalk, happy and relieved to see me.

"Thank you for coming down here, Lucy. How did you sleep?" Nicholas opened the door to the bar and allowed me to walk in.

"Horribly," I replied as I glanced at him shyly. I noticed that he hadn't shaven and that he looked pretty tired himself.

"I'm sorry to hear that. We've been here all night, combing the place for fingerprints. Charles has been very cooperative and has provided us with some helpful information. Apparently, Jimmy spent a lot of time at this bar."

"How is Charles? What's going on? Is he under arrest?" I asked anxiously.

"We released him late last night. He promised not to leave Boston and was going to return to his apartment. He is eager to help, but I'm not sure he can be trusted. We did learn that Jimmy left this bar two nights ago with a woman. The bartender waited on them and said that they looked oddly close. He felt the woman was way out of Jimmy's league, but she left with him anyway."

"Was it Kathryn?" My heart sank at the idea. Whoever killed Jimmy may have Kathryn in their custody.

"The bartender looked at some pictures of Kathryn and he says it was absolutely not her. He said the girl's name was Annie. Does that ring a bell with you?"

I breathed a big sigh of relief. "No, I've never heard of Kathryn talk about an Annie before."

"We've confiscated the video cameras in the bar area and at the marina. Hopefully we can successfully identify this woman and bring her in for questioning."

I nodded as Nicholas spoke, my mind spinning from all the information. I wanted desperately to talk to Charles. I knew that if I could speak with him, I could reassure myself that he was innocent of any wrongdoing. Nicholas sat close to me at the bar, watching me think, his expression full of concern.

"What is it, Lucy? What's on your mind? You can talk to me; I'm here for you."

I looked at Nicholas, his strong, authoritative figure so supportive. I felt so safe with him. His badass Boston accent and attitude, you could tell he grew up on the streets. But yet, he was kind and easy to be with. I just wanted to find Kathryn. I questioned how I kept finding myself in these hugely emotional situations. This past year has been such a rollercoaster. I wanted to confide in Nicholas, but I couldn't tell him these things; he barely knew me.

"I'd like to see Charles. I'd like to talk with him." *Please end this nightmare for me. Find my sister and send us back home, happy and healthy.*

Nicholas looked into my eyes. He considered my request carefully. He reluctantly agreed to bring me back to Charles and Kat's apartment.

"I'm going with you," he stated firmly.

I grinned at him with wide eyes. "I appreciate that, really. I hate to take your time away from the investigation." I mentioned this knowing that my safety was just as important to him.

"To be honest, I would like to see his reaction toward you. It's very telling, someone's body language. One thing is for sure; you're not going alone. He's still considered a suspect." I took a deep breath and closed my eyes for a second. I opened them quickly and Nicholas was staring at me, a look of sympathy on his face. He smiled, embarrassed by our intimate moment. Perhaps it was just my imagination. I felt so vulnerable and he seemed so strong.

"Come with me. I'll drive you to your sister's."

I followed Nicholas as we left the bar. He stopped and talked with another detective working on the case. The officers around us stopped and listened with respect and attention. Nicholas spoke with authority, commanding the room and people around him, smartly assigning the list of tasks that they still needed to complete. He was an impressive man. He was very interesting.

I followed him to the black SUV waiting at the curb. He opened the door for me as I climbed in. I watched him walk around the car.

Interesting, very interesting.

CHAPTER 39

Kathryn

Kat wasn't sure how it happened; her mind couldn't decide what to think. Now she lay here, her eyes covered and bandaged and her wrists tied together, incapacitated and unable to move. She had been crying for hours. Her tears burned through the fabric that was wrapped so tightly around her head. She knew where she was. The scent and smell was unmistakable, but yet she still couldn't believe it. She couldn't understand it. She felt so hurt, so deceived.

A knot formed in her throat and her stomach turned, threatening to vomit. She tried hard to calm herself but it was so difficult; all she could do was cry. The image of it still burned in her head.

Sam. She was dead.

Kat could feel her lip quiver as she thought about her. Sam was so confused, so angry. She killed Jimmy and she would have killed her. Kat still couldn't believe it. Sam was dead. It didn't make any sense. It was so gruesome, how it all ended.

She whimpered in discomfort as she moved her wrists back and forth, the pain of the rope cutting through her skin. She sobbed loudly. She knew no one could hear her. What was she going to do? This couldn't be the end for her. How could this have happened?

She went over the chain of events in her mind. Kat did what she was told. Sam and Kat sat on the T for what seemed like hours while Sam tried to figure out what they were going to do. Sam said she had a plan. When they got off the T, they took a taxicab to the airport, where Sam could rent a car. Her plan was to go up north. No one knew about her, no one from Kat's family anyway. No one knew Sam was in Boston. Sam said that she was confident that Kat could disappear with her and that no one would ever know the difference. They would suspect that Charles had killed Jimmy in some sort of jealous rage and that Charles killed Kat and hid her body. Sam bragged about her brilliant plan; she was proud of her deception.

Kat was buying herself time. She knew eventually that Sam would let her guard down. It might take a week or two, but

Kat would escape from her clutches. Sam couldn't keep her forever. She wasn't a cold-hearted person, it sounded like she killed Jimmy in self-defense. Kat tried to convince her to go to the police, but Sam was scared.

They drove up north and Sam rented a cabin in the woods. The small lodge had two rooms and a bathroom. Sam had nervously tied Kat's hands together and confined her to the living room of the cabin, while she paced the bedroom making phone calls. Kat could hear her trying to arrange an escape route through Canada. Kat wasn't sure if Sam was seriously going to go through with this. Kat refused to speak to her. If she was going to be held her prisoner, then she wasn't going to communicate with her. It was frustrating and made Sam anxious.

While Sam was trying to figure out an escape route, Kat was trying to figure out hers. The cabin had basic necessities: a couch, a small kitchen and a bed in the bedroom. There were two windows in the front of the cabin and two windows in the back. Kat could see that woods surrounded them on all sides. She knew the driveway was in the front of the cabin. That would be her way out; she would need to follow it to the road.

When she thought about this now, none of it mattered. Her head hurt as she recalled the events of the evening. She remembered Sam laying her down on the bed to go to sleep. Kat was exhausted and thinking about Charles and Jimmy. She thought she would never sleep again, but she did. She needed the rest to clear her head.

At some point in the night, she could hear the dogs barking. It sounded like mad wolves were surrounding the cabin. Kat thought it could be the police. She was hopeful that they had tracked them down and this whole weird kidnapping would be over.

Sam jumped out of bed and ran around the cabin, carefully looking through the windows to the outside. She grabbed her gun and loaded it. She sat Kat up in the bed and got their things ready to leave. Kat's heart was racing as she listened to the dogs come closer and closer. Sam continued to nervously look out of every window. "I can't see them. I can't see anything," she repeated again and again. Kat suggested that maybe it was a pack of wolves making a kill nearby. The noises sounded so close, so fierce, but sometimes, it didn't. Sometimes it sounded like it was in the distance.

Sam carefully opened the front door and walked out onto the small porch. Kat held her breath, hoping to see the bright lights of police cars and police dogs barking. What came next she could never have imagined.

A pack of dogs, four or five in total, came flying around the corner, taking Sam completely off guard as they jumped on her, knocking her to the ground. Kat could hear her screaming for help as she recklessly shot her gun, trying to scare the animals. One dog squealed in pain—she must have shot it amid the chaos.

Kat lunged and slammed shut the front door to keep the dogs from running into the cabin. She watched from the window as they mauled Sam, continuously ripping at her body, quickly quieting her screams until she no longer moved. The wild dogs continued to pull at her, their faces covered with blood and flesh, their teeth exposed as they growled and bit at each other while they fought over her mangled body.

Sam was dead.

Kat heard a whistle. Instantly, the dogs stopped their ferocious attack and ran from the porch and disappeared into the darkness. Kat stepped back from the window, scared and uncertain.

She wanted to run on the porch to see if she could help Sam. She wanted to run and grab her gun, but her hands were still tied. She looked around the cabin quickly for a knife or a sharp object. She frantically moved around, using her tied hands to open drawers and cabinets. Lucky for Kat, Sam was careless in her ability to tie a strong knot. Kat worked the rope against the side of the counter and it began to slowly loosen, relieving her wrists of the restraints. With her arms and hands free, she quickly scanned the windows for any movement from outside. She couldn't see the dogs and she could no longer hear the barking. Kat closed her eyes briefly as she prepared herself to open the front door.

What she saw, she could never forget.

The person standing on the porch, the man in charge of the dogs responsible for Sam's murder, she could never forgive.

Her mind went blank as she felt her body fall to the floor.

Now she was here, again kidnapped and imprisoned. It was like a bad dream that kept playing, over and over again. Except, this time, she may not survive. This time, she knew she might die.

CHAPTER 40

Lucy

I followed Detective Nicholas down the sidewalk toward my sister's apartment building. I wasn't sure how I was going to react, seeing Charles. I was nervous to find out. I looked around the hardened street at the onlookers that have formed around the police presence. A few young kids ran up to greet us, calling Nicholas by his first name. He stopped to speak to several of the kids, showing concern and interest into their lives and what they were up to.

"How's it going, boys? How's school, you kids playing ball?"

Several of the boys spoke rapidly, eager to inform him of their good grades and after-school activities. One little boy lingered in the back, shy and quiet but observing Detective

Nicholas. Nick walked through the group of kids and bent down to speak to the little one, perhaps eight years old. The young boy's face lit up as he smiled, warming my heart as I watched the exchange take place. Nick shook the little boy's hand. An agreement was made, although I couldn't quiet hear the details. I looked around the street and was feeling far more secure than the first time I drove down this road. It was still hard for me to understand why my sister lived here, but I could see the children and their faces now. They were just kids, normal kids trying to survive in a rough neighborhood.

Detective Nicholas said goodbye to the children and we began to walk toward Kat's building.

"What was that all about?" I asked, nodding my head toward the youngest boy.

Detective Nick looked into my eyes. "He's got it rough, that boy. His mother is a heroin addict, constantly in trouble with the law. He lives with his grandmother now, a few houses down from here. He's a good kid; he looks after his siblings. If he gets straight A's this semester, I promised him I'd take him to a ball game." I watched Detective Nicholas as we continued to walk. What he did for people was meaningful, he paid attention.

As we approached Kat's, I took a deep breath and followed Nicholas into the first set of doors toward the apartment. I began to prepare the questions in my head. The questions Nicholas and I discussed on the ride over. Nicholas' concern and determination was obvious. I silently prayed Charles wasn't involved in my sister's disappearance. All this time we spent with him, all the support we shared in our pursuit to find Jack. Maybe it was all for nothing. Jack abandoned me; why not Charles? Maybe they really weren't the people who they pretended to be. How could Kat and I be so stupid, so easily fooled? None of this made sense.

Nicholas knocked twice on the apartment door and Charles quickly ripped it open to let us in. I took one look at him and I was convinced.

"Lucy!"

Charles quickly pushed Detective Nicholas out of his path and pulled me into a strong embrace, his arms wrapped tightly around me like he may never let me go.

I started to cry. So many emotions bottled up, desperately wanting to be released as they came pouring out of me. Charles grabbed my shoulders and held me at arm's length as he looked into my face.

264

"Lucy, Jimmy's dead. We need to find Kat. She's gone! She just disappeared into thin air. I don't understand it. We need to find her!" Charles choked on his words as he shook his head in disbelief. His face was unshaven and his hair completely disheveled. He looked like he had been awake for days. His face was ravaged with pain and helplessness. I knew he didn't harm Kat. There was no way I could believe it. He started to cry and we stood there in the kitchen, embraced, tearful.

I began to gather myself as I tried to remember the questions that I was supposed to ask. Detective Nicholas took one look at me and asked me to sit down at the table. I'm not sure that he's convinced that I'm cut out for detective work.

"Charles? Please, sit with me," I asked as we moved across the room.

Charles composed himself as the three of us sat at the table and began to talk. Charles was unable to release my hand, so I held it tight. I thought about him, alone in this apartment, suffering from the anguish and torment of Kat's disappearance. I thought about Charles, arrested and confused over Jimmy's death. He must have felt so alone, so helpless, so scared.

"Charles, I'm not going to leave you now. I'll stay here with you until we figure it out. Until we find Kat. We can do this together."

Nicholas looked at me as I talked to Charles; a concerned look crossed over his face. I'm sure he would prefer I stay with my brother, but Thomas hadn't come back to Boston yet. When he does, I'm sure we'll all stay together. I couldn't leave Charles now, not like this.

"Lucy, you must believe me that I had nothing to do with this. I can't believe this is all happening." Charles spoke directly to me, ignoring the detective purposely as we spoke.

"I believe you, Charles. I believe you. Can you tell me what you did that day? What happened?" I asked, still gripping Charles' hand.

Detective Nicholas, once again, took out his pad and pencil and began to document our conversation. He hadn't spoken other than to ask me to sit down. He had been eagerly observing our communication and watching my eyes, as I would glance from him to Charles.

"Kat and I spent the night together. It was a perfect night. I love your sister, Lucy. I could never, ever harm her. I just want to find her!" Charles choked up again as he spoke. "We spent the night and then I went to work around five in the morning, which is what I always do. I walked down the street and got on the T and headed for the marina. Nothing was unusual. Everything was how it always was. Jimmy hadn't come home the night before, but that wasn't unusual either. He often stayed out all night, sometimes he slept on the boat." Charles looked directly at the detective. "He drank a lot."

"Yes, I understand," Nicholas said to Charles as he nodded his head.

"When I got to the boat, I saw him there, covered with blood, laying on the boat deck, lifeless, dead. I immediately called the police. I wasn't thinking about Kat, I was thinking about Jimmy. I thought he must have had a run-in last night, perhaps someone at the bar tried to rob him. When the police came and started asking me questions, I decided I better get Kat and make her aware that Jimmy was dead. Kat could vouch for me; I was with her all night. When I called her and she didn't answer, I started to get nervous. I went to our apartment. Kat was gone. There was no note and no reason for her to be out this early in the morning. I started to panic and asked the police to help me, but then the police put me into custody." Charles glanced over at Nicholas and gave him a disgusted look.

"We had to take precautions, Charles. It's a matter of routine," Nicholas replied to his glare.

Charles glanced back at me, his posture rigid and assertive. "So, now here we are, with no leads and no answers."

Detected Nicholas had been continually watching me, observing our interaction. "Well, it's obvious, Lucy, that you trust Charles."

"Yes, I do. I believe him."

Nicholas nodded his head as our eyes locked, reinforcing our understanding.

"Charles, we believe that Jimmy was with a woman the night he was murdered. We have confirmed it with the bartender at the pub. My lieutenant is waiting for the video, which we can view together. Perhaps you will know the woman and could provide us with some insightful information. I would be grateful for your help." Nicholas stood from his chair and looked at me as he got ready to leave. "Lucy, I would appreciate it if you could still assist me today, with the investigation."

I glanced over at Charles; a panicked look crossed over his face.

"I need to do something. I can't sit here all day, waiting!" Charles argued, exhausted by the day's current events.

"Charles, as soon as I get the video, I will call you down to the station. I need you, I definitely need you, but you need to get some rest. You look exhausted." Detective Nicholas put an affectionate hand on his shoulder, offering him strength and support.

"He's right, Charles. You need to shower, shave, and rest. You'll be far more effective with the investigation if you have a clear head," I said lovingly.

Charles looked at us and sighed deeply. "You're right, I can hardly stand anymore. Those bed cots you keep down at the holding cell aren't exactly comfortable."

I walked Charles into my sister's bedroom and helped him lay on the bed. I covered him with a blanket and kissed him on his face. "I promise, Charles, I'll call you if we hear anything significant. As soon as the video becomes available, we will come back and pick you up so we can view it together. Just sleep for a little while, it's important."

"Okay." Charles leaned his head back and his eyes instantly closed.

I began to turn to leave the room when Charles quickly grabbed my arm and pulled me back to him.

"Find her, Lucy. I know you can find her. I need her. She's all I have."

A knot quickly formed in the back of my throat as I watched Charles give in to his exhaustion.

I walked back into the kitchen where Detective Nicholas was waiting for me. I felt so helpless, so vulnerable. I could feel my positive outlook collapse into a pile of overwhelming concern and discouragement. I looked at the detective, my face crumbling, my heart devastated as I thought about Kat, alone and scared somewhere, with no one. He looked at me, uncertain of how to comfort me. Our time together was personal, the detective and I. There was no other way to be, but close. It was our mission to find Kat, the ultimate bonding experience. He held his hand out to mine and I slowly walked into him as he embraced me with gentleness, with kindness.

"This is a lot to handle, for a little girl," he said quietly.

I started to laugh through my tears.

"I'm not a little girl." I wiped my face on his shirt.

"I know you're not," he said with affection.

270

I hugged him tightly. I felt safe. I felt protected. I liked being close to him. His strength helped me.

"Are you ready to go?" Nicholas asked. I didn't want to let go; I wanted to forget for another minute. I pulled myself away from his embrace and grabbed my purse.

"I'm ready."

CHAPTER 41

Kathryn

Kathryn vaguely remembered hitting the porch floor of the cabin as her mind blanked from the shock of what she just witnessed. She tried to gather her thoughts as she was being picked up off the floor and carried away into the vehicle. Her eyes fluttered as she tried to speak, rolling back into her head; they were unable to focus. She couldn't control her body. Her head and mind were spinning, the only thing she could do was to give in to it and sleep. She must have slept for hours because when she awoke she was locked into her old bedroom, hands tied and bound like a criminal.

She needed to find her voice, but it was so difficult and her mind was unable to comprehend. He was her best friend—how did it come to this? She begged him. She begged him to talk to her, explain this to her. How did he find them? What about the dogs? He sat for hours at her bedside and cried, his hands running over his face, his words lost to anger.

"Please, Demetry. Please loosen my restraints. I want to talk with you, but this is painful."

He stared at her blankly while she continued to beg him. He walked nervously back and forth from the kitchen to the bedroom.

"I don't understand why you're doing this. It doesn't make sense. What did I do? Why?" Kat asked desperately.

Demetry sat in the chair next to her bed and placed his hand on her forehead. "I didn't want this to be this way, Kat. You have to believe me. I thought we would marry someday. I knew you and Sam would never work out. I thought it was just a matter of time and that you would come to your senses." Demetry stopped talking and stared at Kat with a look of disappointment. "Why did you leave me? And that fucking Sam, she was going to go to the police. I couldn't have that, Kat. I've worked hard for what I've accomplished. I wasn't going to let that bitch ruin everything. And *you!* You just up and leave after everything I've done for you. You never thought about me."

Kat looked at Demetry in shock. She felt so sad for him. How could she be so naive?

"Demetry, I had no idea you felt this way. Why didn't you talk to me? Why didn't you tell me?"

Demetry stood again and began to pace the room.

"Why were you in Boston?" Kat asked, her voice shaken from their conversation.

"I was afraid for you. The day I drove up to visit you, the day you *refused* to come home with me, I decided to hang out for a while and keep an eye on you. That's when I saw Sam. She had been watching you too. She was following you everywhere. So I decided to stay."

As Demetry spoke, it began to register. Kat had involved herself with two very fucking crazy people. How did she not see this coming?

"Sam killed Jimmy," Demetry confirmed. A look of acknowledgement spread across Kat's face. "Obviously, she must have confessed to you. They've arrested Charles for his murder."

Kat could feel herself falling off a steep cliff, her stomach dropping as she listened to Demetry reveal that information. It was exactly how Sam planned it. She knew that

274

they would arrest Charles and that there would be nothing Kat could do about it.

"Demetry, please. You can't keep me here. This isn't right. I appreciate that you saved me from Sam, but you have to let me go. I don't love you, Demetry. Not in that way."

Wrong words to say.

"Fuck you, Kat!" Demetry screamed his words at her as he stood and walked back into the kitchen. He began to throw glassware and dishes onto the ground, shattering them. He began banging the kitchen cabinets, angrily shutting them, mumbling words of resentment to himself.

Kat lay in the bed, unable to see but able to hear the ruckus he was making. She shook her head as the thoughts of Charles sitting in a jail cell came to her. Charles had no idea what was happening. She felt so helpless.

Demetry came back into her bedroom and unleashed her hands.

"What are you doing?" she asked.

"You're going to the basement," he responded unemotionally.

"No, Demetry! Please, let me go!"

"Sorry Kat, but you asked for this. This is all your fault."

Kat cried and pleaded as Demetry walked her down the stairs to the basement, kicking and screaming. He opened a door, a door she had never been allowed in. She always thought he had drug supplies and materials in this room. Demetry removed the wrappings around her eyes and she could feel the fear run through her stomach, up her chest, and into her arms as she looked around the room.

Pictures hung everywhere: pictures of her gardening, pictures of Sam and her. Intimate pictures of time they've spent in her bedroom. She was terrified and she couldn't speak. She could feel his eyes on her, watching her reaction to the wall of photos. He was crazy. He was absolutely crazy.

Demetry forced her back down on the bed and tied her hands and covered her eyes. She felt defeated. She had no more strength at this point. The thoughts invading her head were overwhelming; she wanted to stop him. She wished she were stronger than him, that she could escape him. She was helpless.

She could hear the dogs, they sounded like they were in the basement. She knew Demetry's mother had dogs and that she trained them. But she never knew they were attack dogs. This was crazy. She really knew nothing about him.

"If you try to leave, Kat, the dogs will kill you. They are just outside this room. I wouldn't risk it if I were you. You know what happened to Sam."

She was barely listening. She wanted to sleep at this point; she was so exhausted.

Demetry knelt down and kissed her lips. She wanted to vomit.

He left her now. He was gone. She didn't know if he would come back.

One thought dominated her mind.

She was going to die here, in this basement, with a bunch of killer fucking dogs.

CHAPTER 42

Lucy

Detective Nicholas and I decided to return to the bar and walk to the marina to examine the boat. Although Nicholas wanted my help with the investigation, he was protective regarding what I saw and how much information I knew. I'm not really sure why he needed me with him, but I was grateful to be doing something useful. I felt a pull toward Nicholas; he was a distraction from my thoughts of Jack. It seemed odd but I felt that Nicholas needed me, just as I needed to be distracted. He was someone that I would date, I realized; he was a strong man and I held respect for the way he was handling my sister's case. There was something sweet about him, the way he cared and spoke to the children on the street. Although we hadn't spent much time together, he seemed to know what I needed from him. I needed someone to care.

As we walked down the sidewalk to the bar, I could see the police presence still lingering on the street and all the way toward the marina. I felt a strong urge pulling me to walk straight for the dock. I glanced up at the bar's sign and looked over at the doublewide entrance doors and continued past them. It was obvious where the crime had taken place. Nicholas spoke to a few of the detectives and then we decided to move on. I occasionally saw him glancing at me, his expression quiet and observing. He was increasingly becoming more and more attentive. He guided me with his hand while we walked; he never left my side. I was sure we were starting to cross the lines of inappropriate behavior, but it felt normal and comfortable.

I was calmly anticipating the murder scene I was about to investigate. My mind was busy. Images, voices, and songs were bombarding me. I needed to find a quiet spot so I could focus on the thoughts that were invading my brain. Maybe I could be helpful after all. Maybe I could sort this out and get some sort of lead toward finding my sister. I began to prepare myself to witness something horrific. I felt terribly sad for Jimmy and how he died. Although we didn't have a close relationship, I remembered him fondly.

I walked behind Nicholas as we made our way under the police tape and up the metal boat dock. Our feet boomed on the steel steps as we made our way toward the boat. I could see the fishing vessel up ahead guarded by a police officer and busy with forensic detectives as they continued to gather more evidence and fingerprints. I took several deep breaths as I prepared to see the dead body of my friend, imagining him drenched in blood and gore. I could see Nicholas turning his head several times to look at me, trying to gage my state of mind. I nodded at him, encouraging him to continue, as I believed that I could handle this.

As we approached the boat, the voices in my head were screaming. I could barely concentrate; the thoughts were so heavily distracting. I vaguely remember walking past the boat and continuing down the dock toward the fishing area along the clubhouse. I could hear the waves splashing against the boats as I made my way down. When I reached the fishing area, I stood against the railings and looked out into the deep ocean. I witnessed the seagulls diving into the water, hoping to catch their lunch as the sun came in and out of the clouds. I closed my eyes and concentrated on my thoughts. I shut out all that surrounded me and focused. I tried to remember Anna's words. "It takes practice," she'd said to me. "It takes practice."

I prayed silently to my mother. I prayed to Sarah for help. I could feel my body sway as if I were sleeping, standing against the railing, the weight of my body being held up miraculously by the air of the ocean breeze.

The vision started and I could see the dogs running through the woods, the man closely behind them, guiding them. My pulse was rapid as I watched them from the trees, going toward the cabin. They listened to him, the dogs. He controlled them.

Sarah filtered in and out of my thoughts. She wanted me to hurry. She was impatient and anxious. I felt the anxiety all over my body. She was not relaxed as she usually appeared. She was nervous.

I pulled myself out of my trance and opened my eyes and focused on the ocean. I felt my heart fill with the fear and the unfortunate acknowledgement that I thought that someone else had died. Nothing made sense, the dogs and the dreams. Practicing wasn't helping my ability to figure out what these visions meant or the hidden secrets that were within them. It was so frustrating. One thing was clear: My mother was anxiously waiting for me to find Kathryn. This thought filled me with hope that she was still alive.

I cleared my head and turned back to look toward the boat. I realized Nicholas was with me, standing against the railings, watching me closely. I remained frozen in my spot, staring at him, unsure of how long I'd been standing there, oblivious. How long has he been watching and waiting? I needed to explain, but I was uncertain what he would think.

He stared and waited for me to speak. His eyes were kind and he showed no signs of judgment. As he leaned against the rails, I watched his face. His tanned and muscular arms folded casually across his chest. His eyes quietly watching me, his body language confident and secure. I opened my mouth, but nothing came out. I needed courage.

"Another woman's been murdered," I blurted suddenly.

Nicholas looked at me, puzzled and stunned by my outburst.

"She appears to be in the woods somewhere, but I don't know where. Dogs! The dogs killed her," I yelled. I knew it sounded crazy. He couldn't possibly understand this. Nicholas walked quickly toward me and grabbed onto my arms and looked into my face.

"We need to talk," he said seriously. He held my arm and he carefully walked me past the boat and down the street to his vehicle. I walked with him, keeping up with his fast pace as he held my hand, guiding me through the streets.

282

I glanced up at him once or twice to see the concerned look glaze over his eyes. *He thinks I'm crazy, I know it.* How could I explain this to him?

Nicholas opened the door to his vehicle and helped me get into the front seat. He closed the door carefully and proceeded to get into the car and started it. He pulled the vehicle into the deserted alleyway alongside the bar and turned off the motor. He turned to face me, his expression grave. My heart was racing. I had only confessed my abilities to Anna and Amelia. What could I say to him, to make him understand? I was so nervous, and I didn't want to waste more time explaining.

"I don't understand," he said impatiently.

"I know this is very difficult to explain," I began.

"You know that someone else has been murdered? How do you know this?" He was suspicious.

"I saw it." I paused, trying to get the strength to tell him. "I saw it in a vision."

Nicholas looked at me carefully as he slowly leaned back into his leather seat. I watched him. I watched to see his expression, but nothing changed. His face remained the same.

"You saw it in a vision?" he asked. "You see things, like a medium?"

"Yes." I sighed. Thank god, he knows what that means.

"You're a medium?" he asked again, making sure he understood me correctly.

I smiled at him slightly. "It's a long story, but apparently when my mother died, she left me a gift. I've been blessed with insight and intuition ever since. I am confused by it and I struggle to understand it, but I'm trying to grasp it and interpret the messages that I receive. Back there, at the boat, I saw someone getting mauled by dogs. I don't know what that means, but it feels very real."

Nicholas looked at me finally, his face full of understanding and acceptance. He held my hands in his as he began to speak. "We've found a body, a body of a woman. Some wild animals, possibly dogs, apparently attacked her." Nicholas paused as he considered sharing the final bit of information. "She's dead, Lucy. They found her body in the deep woods of Vermont. We believe she killed Jimmy. I think we need to take a ride up north. Can you come with me?"

I thought about the information he had just shared with me. I couldn't believe it; I couldn't believe that the vision was real.

"Absolutely," I said. "You don't think I'm crazy?"

"I don't think you're crazy, I think you're special," Nicholas stated softly as he started the truck. He quickly sped down the alleyway onto the streets of Boston. We headed directly for the interstate and started our journey up north toward Vermont. I felt relief, a great burden lifted from my soul. I looked at Nicholas as he drove.

I felt safe.

CHAPTER 43

Lucy

Driving in a large SUV with a Boston detective had its advantages when you were trying to reach a destination in a hurry. Detective Nicholas turned on the vehicles flashing lights and we were able to speed our way up Route 91 into Vermont.

I sat quietly next to him as I listened to him communicate with the other detectives and officers regarding our case. I wanted to ask him questions about himself. I wanted to know things about him—where did he come from? What was his story?

"They've gotten the video," he said, pleased. "We'll view it immediately when we arrive back in town. I sent a detective to notify Charles and to assist him back to the police station.

Perhaps you or Charles will be able to recognize the woman and possibly enlighten us with more information about her."

"That's great news! I felt so guilty leaving Charles. I'm glad he'll be able to help us now. I know how helpless he must feel. I really appreciate you dragging me along with you during this investigation. If I were sitting around doing nothing, I would be going crazy at this point."

Detective Nicholas glanced over at me with a grin on his face. "You *are* crazy, or you would be *going* crazy?" he asked.

I started to laugh as I hit him on his arm. "I knew you thought I was crazy!" I accused.

"No, I don't. I'm just teasing you," he replied.

I smiled at him, embarrassed by his attention. "You're so serious, I like it when you laugh," I stated affectionately.

Nicholas glanced at me quickly, trying to keep his eyes on the road. "You've been a tremendous help to me, thank you."

"Are you from Boston?" I asked, trying to open a more personal conversation.

"Originally, no. I grew up in Pennsylvania until I reached high school. My father past away and my mother remarried, then we relocated to Boston. I finished high school and quickly enrolled in the police academy. My stepfather was a Boston detective and helped pave the way for my career in many ways. He was a great man. He died last year from a heart attack."

"Oh, I'm sorry to hear that." I could hear the sadness in his tone and I understood deeply how he felt.

"Thank you. It was a devastating loss for my mother. She still struggles with it. I try to spend time with her, every chance I get."

I placed my hand on his arm comfortingly. "That must explain why you don't have a heavy Boston accent. I mean, you have one, but it's not like the others."

"I know, it's a little broken," he said with a smile.

"Do you have other siblings?"

"Yes, I do. I have a very large family. I'm the youngest and have three older sisters, all of whom live in the Boston area. They are constantly with my mother, so I am fortunate for that. I also have aunts and uncles and cousins living up and down the New England coast."

I smiled at him while he spoke about his relatives. He became increasingly animated and passionate. I could sense that he had a great love for his family.

"Your family sounds like mine."

"Yeah, it's nice to have a large support system. It helps to get you through the hard times."

I listened as I stared quietly out of the car window. I thought about Kat and my heart broke. I couldn't imagine my family going through another devastating loss. I needed my sister back.

"We'll find Kat," Nicholas stated delicately, as though he read my thoughts. I smiled briefly at him as we pulled off the highway exit and headed north.

"The cabin is only five miles from here. Perhaps you'll be able to sense something from the surroundings. Perhaps Kat was here," he suggested.

"I'll try my best. I don't always control my thoughts or the images. They just come."

Nicholas nodded.

"I'm glad you know my secret. It haunts me. I'm very grateful for your understanding."

"I've worked with mediums before," Nicholas said. "I find it fascinating. I'm glad you trust me enough to share your secret. I feel compelled to help you and your family. I think we work well together and you make me feel very comfortable. I hope when this is all over that we will remain friends, Lucy. I'd like to spend more time with you."

My thoughts were wild as he spoke. It was hard to think about the future when my sister was missing, and with Jack still strongly on my mind. Detective Nicholas, however…he was so interesting, he was so different from anyone I've ever met. I could feel myself wanting his attention. His attitude was so reserved at times, yet he always appeared cool, like a mobster, but on the good side of the law. I wanted to follow him around, to see what would happen next. He made me blush and stumble on my words. I was attracted to his rough appearance, the tattoos and his accent. I didn't feel like he gave everyone his attention, but those who received it felt special. There was a definite, unspoken attraction and concern for one another.

"I'd like that too," I replied with certainty. I wondered if I should dare care for another man again. I wondered if I had the courage.

Nicholas pulled off the road and started his descent down a rocky, dirt driveway leading toward the deserted cabin.

A local police officer stopped us as we drove through the wooded area. Nicholas declared who he was and asked to meet with the lead detective. The police officer allowed us to continue down the road and Nicholas pulled over in a designated area off the side of the driveway.

"Stay here while I speak to the detective. Okay, Lucy?"

"No problem," I replied. I looked around the surrounding area heavily dominated by woods. I watched Nicholas walk across the lawn and shake hands with the other detective leading the case of the murdered woman. I could feel the heat rising from my body as I looked around the vicinity. I leaned over and rolled down the window so I could get some air. I imagined the dogs running across the lawn and attacking the poor girl. There was no indication in the dream that my sister was here, but I think that she was. I felt that she was with the man. Who are these people and why is my sister involved with them?

Nicholas disappeared with the detective into the small cabin. I decided to get out of the truck and walk around the wooded area, hoping for some insight. I made my way to a small clearing. I could feel my body get heavy with anxiety. I stood still within the clearing and closed my eyes. I waited for the world to quiet, for my surroundings to disappear, for the thoughts to invade my head.

Sarah walked quickly through the woods toward me, a look of desperation on her face.

"Hurry, Lucy. Go to her," she said.

"Where? Where is she?" I asked.

Sarah glided past me, through the trees. She didn't look back.

"Sarah! Sarah, tell me!"

She was gone.

I turned back to look at the cabin. I saw Kat. I saw her. I yelled for her, but she couldn't hear me. My voice was lost in the dream as I watched her look at the man standing in front of her. I watched her as she fell to the ground.

I fell to the ground, unconscious. I felt the weight of my body hit the cold, damp earth of the forest floor. I stayed this way, my mind numb from my thoughts and my brain frozen still from my dream state of awareness.

I vaguely heard the officer's voices as they scrambled around the trees coming toward my motionless body. I could hear his voice, Detective Nicholas. He was shouting at everyone to stay out of his way. He rushed to my side and I could feel him pick up my body with ease. I wrapped my arms around his neck and slowly brought my thoughts around to my reality and current circumstance.

Nicholas whispered to me, "Are you okay?"

I nodded my head yes.

"We're leaving." He carefully placed me back inside his car and quickly jumped in, backing up the long dirt driveway and out onto the country road heading toward town, leaving a cloud of dust and debris in his wake.

I looked up at him, my eyes focused once again, and I apologized for alarming him.

"You're going home," he stated. "This is too much for you."

"No, Nicholas! You can't do that to me. I saw her. I saw Kat. She fainted on the front porch. There was a man. He's got her. He picked her up and carried her to his car, just like you did for me. Whoever she's with, he's a man and she's very familiar with him."

Nicholas glanced at me, taking all of this information into consideration. He pulled over to the side of the road, his fear, concern, and frustration subsiding. He held his hands tightly on the steering wheel, his knuckles white and scarred, his adrenaline calming, his eyes, penetrating. "Who is he?"

"I don't know, I'm sorry," I said.

He looked carefully at me as I grabbed onto his arm.

"I couldn't see his face," I said, aware of our closeness. I was aware of my desire to please him, to have the right answers, to solve the mystery and to make him proud. I was aware of my desire to touch him. I took a deep breath.

"Go to Boston. Please, Nicholas. We need to find Kat."

The tension between us was thick, intense, hard to ignore. Nicholas slowly sat back into his seat. He carefully put the car in drive and we started back toward the interstate.

Things felt different now between us. Things have changed.

CHAPTER 44

Julia

Julia sat with Amelia in the kitchen as Thomas said his heartfelt goodbyes. He was leaving to get back to Boston, eager to resume his search for Kat. Julia was still trying to wrap her head around the fact that Amelia and Thomas were going to have a baby, let alone about Kat's disappearance. She found it hard to believe that Kat was in any kind of danger. Kat was such a scatterbrain; Julia thought that she was probably sitting around with some harmless environmentalist, discussing how to make the world a better place, unaware that people were out searching for her, looking for her.

Julia looked over at Amelia's face full of worry for her friends. She was such a good soul, Amelia. Julia knew that Amelia and Thomas were young, but she was glad that he had her. It was what he had always wanted. They adored each other. Julia wasn't sure how her father would react to the news of becoming a grandfather, but perhaps it would bring some additional joy into his life. She hoped, anyway.

"What should we do, Julia?" Amelia asked.

"We wait here, I guess. Thomas promised he would call us as soon as he gets to Boston, to let us know what's going on," she replied. "There's not much we can do, Amelia. Perhaps you should take a rest. You look a little tired."

"I just want everyone home, safe and sound."

Julia walked over to Amelia and put her arms around her shoulders. "It'll be alright, Amelia. Everything will be fine."

Julia said those words to comfort her, unsure of the certainty behind them. She closed her eyes and silently prayed, "Dear God, help us."

CHAPTER 45

Lucy

I watched Nicholas as he was eagerly waiting for word from his boss regarding the video from the bar. I gazed at him carefully as we pulled into the police station parking lot. He had a passion for detective work and for helping people. It was obvious; he made the right career path for his life. He loved what he did.

Charles had arrived earlier and was waiting for us. I felt nauseous at the thought of seeing Jimmy again, alive and well, unknowing that he would soon be murdered and left to die. I felt like I was walking around in this weird nightmare, my world so unpredictable now. Bad things didn't happen to people like me, and now bad things kept happening to people like me. It felt unnatural, unbelievable. Kat was so innocent and helpless. She could never hurt a fly, and yet she might have to. The situation was so bizarre.

Nicholas parked and we rushed up the station stairs and into the main reception area. He said hello to several people as the receptionist buzzed the locked security door, allowing us to enter. Nicholas held the door for me and then walked me across the room with his hand on my back. The simple touch of his hand felt different now. I felt like he had a power over me, his assertiveness exciting. I was willingly succumbing to the fact that I liked him.

Detective Nicholas stopped briefly to introduce me to his partner.

"Lucy, this is my partner Alex."

Alex smiled widely as he said hello. "I've heard great things," Alex said. "Hey Nick, can you spare a minute for me? It's really important."

I watched the two men briefly interact. I could tell the way they communicated that they were close, like old high school friends.

"I know it is, Alex, but we're just about to look over some video." Nick pushed past Alex, calmly turning his head toward him. "I promise Alex, you're next on my list, my friend."

I turned back and said goodbye to Alex. I could see the disappointment registering on his face. He wanted Nick's attention and he said it was important.

"I can wait, Nick, if you need to help him."

Nick grinned slightly. "It can wait."

We continued on. I was eager to see Charles. I hoped that he had gotten some rest and felt positive about finding Kathryn.

Nicholas walked me into a quiet viewing room at the back of the police station. The room was dark and full of people. There were several chairs scattered around aimlessly in the front. I saw Charles first, sitting, ready and eager to view the video. I quickly went to him and sat next to him.

"How are you?" I whispered as I held his hand.

"Better, thank you. Any luck?" he asked, hopeful.

"We haven't found her, but I think she's still alive. I feel confident she's still with us."

Charles looked up at me, his eyes despairing.

Nicholas dragged a chair next to mine while two additional officers joined us in the room. A man's voice came over the intercom, asking Detective Nicholas if he was ready. Nicholas waved his hand and leaned over to whisper in my ear, "Are you ready for this? This could be very difficult to watch."

"I'm ready. I know it's important. It needs to be done," I said stoically.

Nicholas stared at me for a moment, looking carefully into my face.

I smiled to reassure him. "I promise, I won't pass out."

Nicholas spoke into his handheld device and notified the officers to start the tape. I could feel my stomach turning, the energy in my body exhausted by all the stress. I had been anticipating watching this tape all day. I started to look around the room; I observed all the people involved in looking for my sister. These people didn't know her, but yet they were all here to help her.

I turned to look, trying to remember so I could thank everyone later. I didn't know why I hadn't noticed before. I didn't know *how* I didn't notice before.

Jack.

He sat quietly, studying the situation, watching me from behind. He waited and held my stare. *I think I might die.* Jack was here. Charles must have called him. I could feel the sweat instantly swarm around my neck and chest as my nerves suddenly sent my body to overheat. I could feel the room enclose and the sudden and sweltering heat left me breathless, as if I were sitting in a steam room.

I nervously turned back around as the video had started to play. How did I not anticipate that Jack would be here? Of course Charles would have called him.

The footage was black and white and somewhat cloudy. The video changed at various locations. Views from the sidewalk in front of the pub, to the hallway entering the pub, then again to the bar area of the pub, filtered through the camera's lenses.

I watched eagerly as the video played. I saw Jimmy. It was raining hard that night. He had his head covered with a jacket to ward off the rain, but I could tell that it was him.

"That's Jimmy."

"I agree," Charles said. "That's definitely him."

The video showed Jimmy entering the inside of the pub and then sitting down at the bar area. He ordered a beer and talked casually with the bartender. It was so strange to watch someone hours maybe moments before their death. I wished I could reach into the video and stop it, stop it all from happening.

A few more individuals entered the bar after him. Then we saw her. The woman. "Annie." She had an umbrella covering her face as she walked down the sidewalk and into the bar. You could tell that it was her; she looked so out of place. She didn't seem to fit in to the bar's atmosphere. She was attractive and petite, pretty in her summer dress and delicate in the way she moved. The men at the bar were rough-looking, local fishermen, stopping in after work for a drink and to watch the ball game. I could feel my fingers clutching the sides of the chair as I watched her sit down at the bar, a few chairs away from Jimmy.

I felt panicked. I glanced over at Charles and his face looked distressed as well. I could feel the anxiety manifesting itself. I wanted to close my eyes but I didn't want to overlook anything. I felt there was something we were missing.

I watched the conversation unfold and the casual flirting that took place. I watched as Jimmy and the woman stood and left the bar. We watched the video reveal them walking down the sidewalk toward the marina. That was it. There was nothing else.

302

"Could you play it again, Nicholas?" I asked, desperate to find something more.

"Absolutely. We can play it as many times as you want." Nicholas spoke into the microphone, asking the officer to play the video again.

"There's got to be more," Charles said.

"I agree. It's all so overwhelming, the video, so fast." Frustration began to build within me.

Nicholas leaned over and put his arm around my shoulder. "Are you alright? We can take a break and look at this later."

"No, I'm fine. We need to figure this out...please."

The video began again. I watched patrons as they walked into the bar and as they sat casually around the tables. The TVs were playing various sports events and several men were sitting around, watching them. I watched the woman walk into the bar and sit next to Jimmy.

That's when I saw something. Someone was watching her. A group of men turned to watch the baseball game on the TV screen and then erupted with excitement as the Red Sox scored the winning run. This man's eyes remained fixed on the

303

woman. He didn't participate in the celebration or enthusiasm of the crowd.

"There, that person. Can you get a closer look at that man? Do you see him, Charles?" I grabbed Charles' arm and pointed to the man I was talking about.

"You can barely see his face," Charles stated.

"There's something about him," I said eagerly.

Nicholas spoke into the microphone and asked the man playing the video to focus in on the gentleman in the grey T-shirt. The video paused, rewound, and then froze on a close-up of the man.

I could feel myself holding my breath as I looked at the man's face closely. It was difficult to get a clear view of the man, but I think I knew who he was. In fact, I definitely knew who the man was. I stood to get a closer look at the screen. I was disgusted as I looked into his eyes. I looked back at Charles. He too stood up and closely examined the screen.

"Son of a bitch!" he stated.

In seconds, the room was cleared and police officers were racing around. Nicholas was shuffling us into his private office.

I felt panic, nothing but panic.

CHAPTER 46

Julia

"It's going to be okay, Dad. They're going to find her safe and sound. I'm sure of it." Julia should have told him sooner. He was not a happy camper.

"You damn kids think you need to protect me from everything that goes on around here. I'm a grown man; I need to know what's happening with my children. This is ridiculous!" Joseph spat. "I need to go to Boston. I belong there, looking for Kat."

"If that's what you want to do, then I'll stay here with the kids."

"I want to go with you," Amelia stated as she stood to grab her purse.

"No, no, no," my father argued as he sat her back down in her chair. "There is no way you are coming with me, not in your condition." Joseph looked affectionately at Amelia as she began to pout, sitting at the kitchen counter.

"Nice try, Amelia," Julia said. "Thomas just brought you back from Boston. Do you really think he would be happy to see you reappear, when it was clear he didn't want you there to begin with?"

Julia watched Amelia and shook her head in disbelief. She knew Amelia wanted to be helpful, but she also needed her to be a little reasonable. The last thing they needed was to worry about her and the baby.

"This is so hard, sitting around here waiting. I feel so helpless," Amelia whined, defeated by her in-law family. "One thing's for sure, I can't sit here all day." Amelia stood again and grabbed her purse as she started for the door.

"Where are you going now, you little pipsqueak?" Joseph asked, distracted by Amelia's dramatics.

"I want to stop by and talk to Demetry. He doesn't know that Kat is missing and I'm sure that he'll be concerned. He should know what's happening. They are very close, Kat and Demetry."

"Are you going to come back here?" Julia asked.

"Of course! What's the alternative? I can't sit around waiting at home, with my mother! No thanks! I'll be back."

"I'm leaving too. I'm going to Boston." Joseph grabbed his keys.

"Alright. Keep me posted, Dad. Bye, Amelia. I'll see you later."

"Bye, Julia!" Amelia said sweetly.

CHAPTER 47

Lucy

"Who's the guy in the video?" Nicholas asked as he shut his office door firmly behind him.

"He was Kat's roommate. His name is Demetry Franco. Please Nicholas, we need to go to Connecticut. I can fill you in on all the details later, but we need to get on the road," I pled.

Nicholas looked at me and picked up the phone while I spoke. He placed a call to the Connecticut State Police and notified them of our situation.

"The state and local police will ride over to his house to investigate. We can meet them there. Who are you?" Nicholas looked across the room over at Jack, who was sitting quietly behind Charles, watching us speak.

"This is my brother Jack," Charles said.

Nicholas nodded to Jack and looked back at Charles. "So, Kat and Demetry lived together? When?"

"She moved out at the beginning of the summer, when we came here to Boston to charter a boat. Kat, Jimmy, and I rented an apartment together."

"Has she ever said anything strange about Demetry? Anything unusual?"

"Demetry and Kat were best friends. I don't understand this. I thought he loved her," I stated as fond memories of the two of them began to flood my thoughts.

"Love can make you do funny things," Jack stated casually. I glared back at him, unable to quite look him in his eyes.

"Well, we don't know if he's committed any crimes yet but it's a lead. It's a definite lead," Nicholas said.

An officer knocked loudly on the office door, opening it slightly and excusing himself for interrupting.

"Detective Nicholas? The sergeant wants to speak to you before you leave. Also, there's a Thomas here asking for Lucy."

"Thank you, Mathew. I'll be there in a minute. Send Thomas to my office. Lucy, you can fill him in and then I will meet you outside."

"Yes, okay. Thank you, Nicholas."

Nicholas left the room in a hurry as I paused to gather myself before I turned to address Charles and Jack. Jack stood immediately and went to my side, eager to speak to me, eager to defend himself, eager to be heard.

"Lucy, I'm so sorry about Kat. If you need me to do anything, anything at all, please ask. I'm here for you and Charles. I want to help."

"Yes, well I'm glad you are here for Charles." I looked over at my sister's boyfriend and watched him as he moved around the office, anxiously. "Will you head back to Connecticut, Charles?"

"What do you think? What if she's not there? What if they're in Boston still? Maybe we should wait. Maybe the state police will be able to tell us something before we drive all the way back to Connecticut. I hate to be wasting time." Charles spoke rapidly as he combed his fingers through his hair. His concerns were worthy of consideration. Kat may not be in Connecticut. In fact, why would she be? It was so close to our home. It didn't make sense.

Thomas knocked on the door and walked into the suddenly cramped office.

"Hey Thomas!" I said as I reached up to hug him. "How's Amelia, is she okay?"

"Yes, she's fine. What's going on with the case? Any possible leads?" Thomas asked impatiently.

"You won't believe who was on the tape the night Jimmy was killed," Charles said.

"Who?"

"Demetry!"

"What do you mean, Demetry?"

"He was in the bar the night Jimmy was killed. He was watching that girl 'Annie.' It was like he was following her."

"What the hell! I'm going to kill that guy! Where is he now?" Thomas asked, ready for a confrontation.

"We were just discussing whether we should all go back to Connecticut, or if some of us should wait here," Charles

312

began. "I guess the local police are on their way to investigate his house. What do you think, Thomas?"

"Jesus Christ, I just got here. I would have stayed home, had I known."

"Well, I don't know what you people plan to do, but I'm going with Nicholas to Connecticut." I moved toward the door.

"Wait a minute, Lucy, let's call Julia. Dad should know what's happening."

Thomas moved around the back of the desk and picked up the phone to dial our house number. Julia answered the phone and Thomas quickly filled her in on the latest in the investigation.

"Thomas, Dad's on his way to Boston and Amelia left here twenty minutes ago. She was heading toward Demetry's house. She wanted to fill him in on Kat's disappearance!"

"What?" Tommy asked, instantly regretful for having left her with Julia.

"She's gone. She went to his house!"

Thomas slammed the phone down.

"Amelia went to Demetry's! I'm going to Connecticut!" He rushed toward the door.

"Oh my god, Thomas. Amelia has no idea, we need to stop her." I panicked and opened the door, tripping over Thomas and colliding with a clerk and her coffee on the other side. "Sorry ma'am, excuse me, pardon me, we need to get through."

We stumbled over each other, rushing outside onto the street. Rain had started to fall and thunder rumbled in the distance. Nicholas instructed us to stay put as he rushed off to get his vehicle.

Jack grabbed my arm and turned me around smoothly as we waited for Nicholas to return.

"I need to speak to you. It's important, Lucy. Please. It will only take a minute," Jack pled.

I covered my head from the steady flow of the rain that fell upon us as I looked into Jack's eyes. "Not now." I moved away from him, not willing to show him the pain that I felt, not willing to give him the satisfaction.

"Please, Lucy. I came all this way to see you. I just want to explain."

I turned to face him once again, anger filling my chest as tears began to escape my eyes. I was grateful for the rain, as it disguised my hurt expression.

"I never asked you to come Jack. You've said enough to me for a lifetime. I'm not interested in listening to you anymore. You've hurt me, Jack. Why, why did you do that? I don't understand it." I could feel my emotions getting the best of me. I could feel him pulling them from me, his effect on me, still strong and powerful.

"I was scared," Jack said softly. "I regretted sending that letter to you, the instant I mailed it. I'm sorry, Lucy. I can't take it back, but please, you need to forgive me. It was a great mistake. I was so upset and confused. I should have tried harder. I should have waited."

The rain poured down on us as he yelled over the noises of the traffic and the sounds of the loud city and the people that surrounded it. Jack held my arms and looked into my face. My emotions were twisted. He had meant so much to me, for so long. His presence was confusing me. It was difficult to feel so much anger when his body and his face were so close to mine.

"I can't think about this, Jack. I want to focus on Kat and Amelia. That's all I can do for now."

"Oh, really? What about Nicholas? I see how he looks at you. It's obvious, Lucy."

Nicholas pulled his car up next to the curb and I could see his lights shining down on us as he climbed out of his truck.

Jack still had his hands on my arms as he glanced up toward Nicholas. Jack's eyes locking with his, his stare aggressive and assured.

"Is there a problem here?" Nicholas asked as he approached us on the sidewalk.

Jack looked back into my face. "I know I made a mistake, Lucy, but you owe it to me to work on this. I know you feel it in your heart. We love each other. You can't ignore that. We deserve a chance."

I looked back at Jack. I tried to remember all the beautiful feelings that we shared. The special and intimate moments that were so strongly embedded in my mind. But I couldn't forget. It was hard to forget the letter. The rejection. The disappointment.

"I need to go. I want to find Kat. We'll talk about this later."

I turned to Nicholas and placed my hand in his as he helped me to the passenger side of his car. I looked back at Jack. His face was crushed, jealousy and anger underlying his emotions. I watched them as Charles, Jack, and Thomas got into the car behind ours. I sat back into my seat and turned to look at Nicholas, who was staring at me.

"You okay?" he asked.

I'll never be okay, my heart was broken, my feelings so confused.

"Yes, let's go."

CHAPTER 48

Amelia

Amelia was thankful for the fresh air. Walking made her feel better. She felt such relief now that Tommy knew she was having a baby. But her thoughts were plagued with worry for Kat. This nightmare with Kat has got to come to an end. It didn't feel real. She felt like they were in some sort of low budget terror movie, and endless unscripted horror flick that was riddled with a staff of innocent victims.

Thomas would find Kat. She was confident that he would.

As she walked down the sidewalk she tried to remember the house Demetry lived in. She glanced at them all, one by one. She vaguely remembered the yellow one. She remembered the gardens because they were nicely manicured and cared for. They appeared overgrown and crowded with weeds now, in desperate need of some attention. She bent down and picked a Black-eyed Susan out of the bunch of flowers littering the fence line. Perhaps it had been too hot to care for Demetry's yard lately. She remembered how cute his little yellow house was. This was going to be a shock to him, finding out about Kat; she hated to be the bearer of bad news.

Amelia glanced down the street and over at the next-door neighbor's yard before she walked up the sidewalk to knock on the front door. The neighborhood was so quiet. She wondered if Tommy and her would live in a house like this someday. They could plant gardens and flowers and raise a happy little family. She hoped she would have a boy. She would love to have a boy.

She knocked on the front door. The metal door vibrated as she banged and rang the doorbell. She waited for the door to open or to hear any sounds coming from within. She heard nothing. She knocked and rang the doorbell again. She saw the curtains move from the kitchen window. She smiled and waved, although she couldn't quite see the person behind the pieces of fabric. The door opened and Demetry was standing there, looking at her, confused.

"Hey, Demetry. I'm not sure if you remember me. My name is Amelia. I am a friend of Lucy's, Kat's sister?"

"What is it?" he said sharply.

"Do you mind if I come in? I need to speak to you."

Demetry hesitated, looking at Amelia with uncertain eyes, but he opened the front door for her. He watched her as she walked past him into the kitchen. He invited her to sit down at the table.

"Thank you so much. I just walked here from Lucy's and it's quite a walk. Do you mind if I ask you for a glass of water?"

Demetry looked at her strangely, suspiciously, then stood and poured her some water. Amelia noticed that he hadn't shaved in some time. His beard had grown long and looked very hot and uncomfortable. The heat this summer had been unbearable; she wondered why he would keep such an unkempt beard. His kitchen looked messy and cluttered. Newspapers littered the table and countertops.

"I came to let you know there's been an accident." How do you tell someone that his or her best friend was missing? It seemed so unreal and unbelievable. "Do you remember our friend Jimmy? He grew up with Kat, in our old neighborhood?"

"Yes, of course, the skinny kid."

320

"Yes that's right." Amelia paused for a moment, considering how to say the words. "Well, he died. The police think he's been murdered. Charles and Kat lived with him in Boston, as I'm sure you know. Is there any chance you might have spoken to Kat lately?" Amelia felt sort of like an investigator. Her tone changed suddenly and seriously, as she wasn't exactly sure how to blurt it all out.

Demetry stood from the table and turned his back away from Amelia, his body language appearing stressed and irritated. "I've been trying to call her. She won't return my calls." Demetry walked around the kitchen nervously, oddly.

"Yes, well we can't find her. She's missing." Amelia watched Demetry as she said the words to him. His face remained still and unchanged. He stared at her blankly. She wasn't even sure that he was listening to her. "We've been looking for her. We believe there's been another murder." She paused and waited for him to react. "Demetry, I know this is hard to understand. It sounds crazy, even to me, but I thought you should know." Amelia stood and began to move from her seat. She didn't like the feeling she was experiencing. She didn't like his look. She wanted to go home now.

"Do they have any leads, the police? Any idea where she might be?" Demetry asked flatly.

"No, they are still looking for her in Boston." Amelia stood near her chair, eager to be sitting back at Lucy's house again with Julia.

"Where are you going?" he asked as Amelia walked to the front door.

"I came to tell you about Kat, but now I must go. Thanks for the water. If I hear any more news, I'll let you know." Amelia turned and grabbed onto the door handle and was about to swing it open when she heard something. It was the faint noise of whining. It sounded like an animal crying. She hesitated slightly and looked back at Demetry.

Suddenly, Amelia felt a heavy blow to the back of her head—unsure, but it felt like something just hit her hard. She stared at Demetry, who was holding onto a baseball bat, dripping with blood. She placed her hand to her head and felt the blood spilling over her fingers. Confusion riddled her mind as she collapsed onto the ground, halfway conscious.

She felt Demetry push her limp body out of his way and shut the door. He picked her up and carried her down the flight of stairs to the basement. He opened a door.

"Demetry," Kat mumbled. "Please, I need help."

Demetry ignored Kat and placed Amelia's petite body onto the cold concrete floor.

"Demetry! Don't leave me, please!" Kat cried.

Amelia vaguely heard the woman pleading. She heard Demetry as he shut the door firmly behind him, locking multiple deadbolts, securely trapping them inside. She glanced over, to her right, wondering where she was and what had just happened. Her vision was blurred. Her body ached all over as a tremendous headache began to pound in her ears. She could feel the hard floor beneath her and she wanted to get up, but she couldn't. She couldn't focus enough or think clearly, her head heavy and confused.

She lay still, willing her eyes to open. She could hear the other person breathing in the room. She wanted desperately to move.

If she didn't open her eyes soon, she would fall asleep. Dammit, open those eyes. She slowly dragged her arm off the floor and it landed hard on her stomach. She tried to remember what just happened. She remembered walking down the street, looking over the neighborhood, thinking about Thomas.

What the hell just happened, where was she? If she didn't start to move, she and her baby would die there. She could feel the steady stream of tears flowing down the side of her cheeks as she thought about her unborn child. She thought about Thomas and the family they were just starting. Her mind was so confused; she couldn't understand why Demetry would want to hurt her.

She tried to move her mouth, tried to make some sort of noise, but it was difficult. She started to mumble; the sounds of a slow steady whimper began to formulate from within her throat. She tried again, harder this time. She groaned louder, unable to verbalize her words; her throat making these sad sounds, like the sounds of a small, beaten, wounded animal being left alone to die.

Kat began to yell, "Who's there? Help me, please! Who is it, I can hear you!"

Amelia heard her words and found immediate comfort and strength when she realized finally that is was the voice of Kat. She knew it was her and she couldn't believe it. Kat was with her, she found Kat! But the danger they were in, what just happened to her?

She tried harder to open her eyes. She could feel no restraints on her body, but for some reason, she still couldn't move her legs. Her head ached and pounded as she tried harder and harder. She whispered, "Kat…Kat."

Kat started to cry. "He's going to kill us if we don't get out of here," she whined. "Please, help me."

"Kat...It's Amelia," she gurgled, her voice barely audible.

CHAPTER 49

Lucy

I looked casually behind me at Tommy's car as we caravanned back to Connecticut, Nicholas' lights flashing as we sped down the interstate. My emotions were exploding inside; my hands visibly shaking as I eagerly anticipated our journey back to my hometown. I shook my hair out and dried my face with a paper towel, thinking about my confrontation with Jack. I could sense Nicholas watching me, waiting for me to gather myself, but I was unable to meet his stare.

I suddenly felt very uncomfortable and on edge. The drive to Connecticut was going to feel awkward; I didn't know how to explain Jack's sudden appearance to him. Nicholas remained quiet for the moment, but I suspected he wanted an explanation. I wasn't sure what to say to him. I couldn't tell if he was irritated about Jack or if he had just put on his game face. We were nothing, Nicholas and I, but there was something, and to try to explain to him my feelings for Jack seemed too preliminary and unimportant. He still remained quiet, silently disappointed as we drove.

The waiting was going to kill me. We couldn't get there fast enough. I was so grateful once again to be with an officer of the law. We were at least able to speed, although the quick maneuvering in and out of vehicles was also making my stomach turn. It didn't matter. I wanted to get to Demetry's. We weren't sure if Demetry was even in Connecticut, or if Kat was with him, but we needed to find out. Now that Amelia may have put herself unknowingly into harm's way, there was no way we could wait for the local police to investigate. I couldn't even begin to think about what may be happening. I just wanted to get there. I wanted to find my sister.

Nicholas continued to press the local police for information. There appeared to be some miscommunication as to the urgency of the situation. I couldn't understand why they weren't helping us.

"Nicholas, why can't they enter the house?" I asked, confused.

"They sent a patrolman over and he knocked on the front door but no one answered. They would need to have reasonable cause to enter the house without a warrant. They don't feel they have any reason."

"They don't understand!" Tears rose up in my throat. They weren't aware of how innocent and naïve Amelia could be, and how people were dying. Demetry may be an extremely dangerous and murderous man.

I sat back into my chair and tried to relax my breathing. If I let my panic take hold of me, I may hyperventilate. I needed to calm myself. Perhaps something would come through for me. Perhaps I could receive a sign of hope. I closed my eyes and relaxed my thoughts.

All I could think about was Jack. He was such a distraction. What was I going to do about Jack? It was so painful, to see him again, to see his face. I glanced up at Nicholas as he quietly focused on driving along the interstate. He was so strong and secure. He was really focused on his career. I dared to think, what kind of life would I have with him, if this thing—whatever it was we had—worked out? He was a detective. He worked long, crazy hours and he had a very dangerous job. Emotions were high right now. We were in the middle of a murder investigation. He felt protective over me. But what would happen when it was all over? *What would happen if we didn't find Kat?* We *had* to find Kat. There was no other outcome for me.

I looked fondly at Nicholas. I wanted to touch his face. I wanted to hug him and hold him and tell him how grateful I was for his help. I reached over and placed my hand on his.

"Thank you, Nicholas, for everything." I glanced down at my hand on top of his. I watched as he followed my stare, his eyes searching mine quickly, his face uncertain as he hesitated.

"Jack? You seem like you have some unfinished business with him."

I took a deep breath. I felt so vulnerable and nervous to express myself to him. Whatever happens between Jack and me…it would never change how I felt about Nicholas. He has given me so much of his time, my family. "It's very complicated, I'm not really sure how I feel right now."

I watched his reaction. I couldn't be the one to put it all out there; I wasn't really sure how Nicholas felt. He stared back at the road, considering his words.

"Do you think about me, Lucy? You know, when we're not together, have you thought about what it would be like, you and I?" He looked over at me again, his eyes penetrating mine.

He was bold. Sweat began to surface beneath my shirt as I thought about Nicholas' intimate question. I was grateful for the damp clothing that I was wearing, drenched still from the rainstorm in Boston.

"Nicholas...If I hadn't thought about you, my life would be less complicated right now and I would be driving in the car with Jack, my brother, and Charles." I held his hand tightly, wrapping my fingers around his, wishing we were alone somewhere private, not looking for my sister.

"I realize you had a life before I met you," he replied. "I realize that our circumstances are far from perfect and that we haven't spent much time together. But if you have any kind of feelings for me, I want you to consider them, because I do have feelings for you. I want to spend more time with you. I want to know more, learn more, and enjoy a nice, calm, quiet meal with you."

I laughed. "What do you mean? You don't want to investigate another murder mystery with me?"

"No...I don't! It's horrible. I can't even focus on my job. I'm so distracted and concerned for your well-being."

"Nicholas, whatever may happen, I want you to know that I will always be grateful for you. I could never thank you enough for what you do. I could never repay you."

"You can, Lucy. You can give me a thought. Please, consider it."

I stared into Nicholas' face, his expression serious and soft. His tone quiet yet forceful. Hi strength and authoritativeness, sexy. I squeezed his hand and watched him drive.

"Thank you, Nicholas."

"You're welcome." Nicholas looked down at his handheld device and answered an incoming phone call. He continued to yell into the phone, bashing the poor officer on the other end, demanding backup when we arrived at our destination. His words were a painful reminder of the dire situation we were in and how time was running out on my family.

Nicholas glanced over at my horrified expression and confidently said, "Let's go get your sister, shall we?"

I grinned carefully, trying not to feel overly confident, but I knew that she would be okay.

I knew we had this.

CHAPTER 50

Kathryn

"Amelia! Amelia!"

Kat sobbed hard as she realized who was in the room with her. A flood of relief filled her as she began to hope that she maybe saved, after all. Then panic began to surface. Amelia's speech was gargled, the strength in her voice concerning.

"Are you hurt?" Kat asked desperately.

"Yes," Amelia whispered.

"Can you move, Amelia?" Kat wildly started to pull at her restraints to loosen them, Amelia's presence giving her the much-needed encouragement to try harder, pull harder and to try to escape from her confinement.

"Kat," she whispered. "My head…"

Kat's heart pounded in her chest. Amelia might be in need of medical attention. Perhaps Demetry had seriously hurt her; maybe one of the dogs had attacked her.

Kat began to rub her head on her pillow, trying to force the blindfold off her eyes. She tried again and again to remove it from her face. She felt it slowly giving away at the back of her head.

Finally, she could see.

Kat looked down toward the floor at Amelia lying awkwardly below her. Her blood-drenched hair was matted to her head. Her face and forehead were covered in dried blood.

"Amelia, I can see you. You're going to be okay, Amelia. I'm here. I'm going to get you out of this place. Stay with me, Amelia. Keep talking, sweetheart. I love to hear you talk. Tell me some stories."

Kat looked down at her hands tied together by rope. She glanced up in the room she was being held captive in. Her stomach muscles began to wrench as she slowly started to realize how sick and demented Demetry's love was for her. She observed his display of pictures. Every inch of available wall space was covered with pictures of her. Intimate pictures of her and Sam hung on the walls. Pictures of her in the garden, pictures of her in the bathroom. Private pictures, nude pictures, everyday pictures. She was horrified at the display. Horrified at the invasion of privacy. Her mind could not comprehend the amount of energy he expended on obtaining these pictures. The amount of stalking she had unwillingly been subjected to for years boggled her mind. Fear seeped into her chest as she realized that all of her secrets would now be public. If anyone found them, they would see the display and she would be forever humiliated. Her secret life would be known to all.

She grew angry. How fucking dare he, that sick motherfucker. She banged her bound hands against the wall, screaming Demetry's name, crying, making accusations and hurdling hurtful words into the air.

"You son of a bitch! I trusted you! I did everything for you!" *How could he do this to me?*

Kat continued to move, determination filling her chest as she started to rub the rope onto itself. She could feel the restraint loosening as she rubbed harder and harder. She pulled at it, her wrists bleeding from the friction tearing at her arms. She closed her eyes and prayed and then pulled one last time. The rope snapped free and flew across the room, smashing against the basement wall, knocking down one of Kat's explicit pictures.

"Good! One down, five hundred more to go," she grunted sarcastically. Kat quickly got off the bed and knelt down next to Amelia.

"Amelia, I'm here. Are you all right? Can you hear me?"

Amelia slightly turned her neck toward Kat. Kat could see the slow, steady flow of blood still escaping the wound on her skull. She jumped up and grabbed the material that had been wrapped around her eyes and placed it over Amelia's wound.

"Try not to move, Amelia. Be still."

Amelia was still unable to open her eyes. She dragged her arm toward Kat and grabbed hold of her hand. She held it weakly.

"The baby," she mumbled.

"What? Amelia? Please, don't move, try to remain still. I don't understand what you're saying."

"The baby!" she said again, forcefully.

Kat sat back on her heels as she started to process what Amelia was trying to tell her. She needed to get them out of there; she needed to find a way.

She looked around the room. There were no windows in this dungeon. She moved to the door and pulled on the handle. The door wouldn't budge. Her only chance of escape was to hope that Demetry came back. She needed to be ready. She looked around the area for a weapon. There was nothing but pictures and a bed. She walked over to the wall of pictures and angrily stared in disbelief. One by one, she swat at the pictures, tearing at them, ripping them down from their prominent display. She swore and cried and released her built-up frustration and fear all over those photos, photos she wanted to burn and hide from the world.

She walked over to the bed and flipped over the mattress. She began to claw at the material and fabric, exposing the broken metal springs that had been stabbing at her for what felt like days. The lose springs broke away with ease as she pulled at several of them. Kat picked up one and touched the thin, tangled metal piece, the sharp end cutting into her skin easily. She began to smile mischievously as she twisted the jagged ends together, winding the pieces in place, creating a strong, pointed piece of metal.

Satisfied with her weapon, she stood before the door and took a deep breath. Her heart was racing rapidly as she stepped forward and began to bang on it.

"Demetry! Demetry!"

She stood, waiting and listening. She began to bang again, screaming even louder, dogs barking at her sudden pounding and obnoxious shrieking.

Finally, she heard his steps. He banged down the cellar stairs, reaching for the locks on the door. She held her breath, the fear in her heart temporarily paralyzing her body into immobility.

She glanced again over at the wall and floor of naked, personal pictures. She glanced down at Amelia. Her skin was pale; blood was still noticeably trickling out of her scalp.

Kat feared she was dying on the concrete surface beside her. She heard the locks and saw the doorknob twisting, Demetry threw the door open in her face.

He stared at her, looking somewhat amazed at her will and determination to free herself from his confinement. Kat stepped back toward the wall as he slowly entered the room, his eyes never leaving hers, his face, twisted with mixed emotions of love, hatred, and guilt.

"I didn't want this to be this way, you have to believe me. I never wanted to hurt you. I never wanted to kill you, but I will. I will, Kat."

Kat stared at the man she never knew, the person who betrayed her so deeply. How was she ever so fooled?

Demetry grabbed Kat by the arm and pulled her toward him, holding her neck in his other hand. Kat winced in pain as he tightened his grip around her throat, restricting her air supply and squeezing her effortlessly. Tears started to run down Demetry's face as he put his cheek up against hers, as he kissed her face delicately, as he smelled her hair for the last time.

He whispered again in her ear, "I never wanted to kill you."

He slowly began to squeeze harder.

Kat knew she would die, she knew this would be it if she didn't save herself.

With all her heart and soul, Kat swung for him, imbedding the sharp instrument into his neck.

Demetry stepped back, clutching at his throat and the sharp instrument. He yanked the weapon out of his neck, his eyes wide with shock at her abrupt and forceful strength. He stepped toward her again—one step, two step...down.

Kat watched his body hit the floor hard and loud, the blood pouring out around his neck and chest. She knelt down near his head and spoke loud and clear: "You motherfucker. You're going to rot in hell."

Keep moving, keep moving.

Kat ran to Amelia and pulled her to her feet.

"Can you walk, Amelia?"

Amelia spoke slowly: "No."

Kat hung onto her hips, carrying her carefully through the basement, scooting swiftly past the barking dogs hiding in the shadows and up the cellar stairs. Amelia's feet dragged, as she was barely able to move.

Kat grabbed the kitchen phone to call for help. No dial tone. She grabbed Demetry's car keys and managed to scream once last time down the basement stairs, "I'm taking your car, ASSHOLE!" She could hear the dogs ferociously barking as she made her way out of the house and into the car. She maneuvered Amelia into the passenger seat. She hurried out of the driveway, sped down the street, and headed for the hospital, praying the entire time.

CHAPTER 51

Lucy

Nicholas and I were first to arrive at the house, though sirens were close nearby. An eerie quietness lingered around the property. I quickly jumped out of the SUV and ran for the front door.

"Lucy, wait!" Nicholas yelled for me.

I swung open the kitchen door and ran into the house, yelling for Kat and Amelia. A trail of blood streamed over the tile floor and down the basement stairs. I followed it, panic ripping at my heart.

"Amelia! Kat! Please, where are you?" I screamed.

"Lucy! Wait one second, for god's sake!" Nicholas entered the house behind me, his gun drawn as he hurriedly investigated the rooms on the first floor.

I was unable to stop myself, hurling my body into the sanctioned room in the basement, tripping over Demetry's dead corpse and landing hard on the concrete floor beside him. My screams of terror summoned Nicholas; he quickly ran down the basement stairs, frantically trying to reach me. He saw me lying on the floor, looking into Demetry's unmoving face. My body trembled with fear as the shock of the dead body rendered me frozen and motionless. Demetry's lifeless eyes stared into mine, a sense of complete sadness filling my soul.

I turned to Nicholas as he pushed past the corpse, quickly picking me up and off the basement floor. I stood there stunned, watching him as he looked around. He bent down to investigate the pool of blood located in the center of the room. He looked at the tossed metal bed and mattress. He stood and looked closely at the display of pictures. He looked up at me.

"They were definitely here," he said, confused.

Nicholas bent down and looked at Demetry, placing his hand on his body and checking for a pulse.

"His body is still warm. We must have just missed them." He stood and walked toward me as I started to back out of the room, my face still full of fear and shock.

"We need to go, Nicholas. They're not here!"

"Lucy, wait. Relax, Lucy, I know you're scared." He reached for my hand. My face was pale and panic-stricken as I continued to walk backward toward the stairwell. I wanted to run, I wanted to run and hide from the disgusting room, from the dead body.

"They're not here!" My panic began to surface, my voice echoing off the damp walls of the basement.

Something was at my back.

I slowly turned to glance down and behind me when my arm was suddenly ripped open. I was dragged to the basement floor, pulled violently along its crevices. I looked blindly into the beast's determined eyes, watching the dog as it twisted and pulled, eagerly trying to gnaw my arm off my body.

I remembered the face. I remembered the angry and violent sounds of growling and whispering, "You're going to pay for this, you little whore. I'll get you...." I have dreamt of this horrifying face for months.

343

My thoughts disappeared as my head hit the concrete floor. I could hear Nicholas yell as he reached for his gun, his voice falling away as I lost myself to unconsciousness.

I looked up at the stairwell. I saw Sarah floating down the stairs in her beautiful white nightgown.

Nicholas drew his gun and began shooting the ravaged animal. The pop, pop, popping sound of the gun was distant and quiet as my mind remained disconnected and out of touch. I could see Sarah clearly as she held out her hand, pulling me toward her. I grabbed hold and floated delicately out of my body, above the crime scene. I witnessed Nicholas picking up my limp figure and carrying me up the flight of stairs. Sarah and I continued after him, Sarah giggling as she smiled at me while we observed the situation unfold.

I felt light and free. I felt no pain. I watched as the local EMTs rushed to assist Nicholas in placing my body on the hospital gurney. I saw Charles, Thomas, and Jack standing on the side, watching the commotion unfolding desperately before their eyes.

Jack eagerly tried to help Nicholas as he continued to yell and scream, keeping Jack at bay. Jack hurried around the EMTs as he tried to reach out to me, yelling.

"Lucy! Lucy! What happened? Is she going to be okay?"

"Stand back, Jack. Stay out of our way!"

Jack's heated exchange of words filled the driveway as Nicholas leapt into the ambulance with me. Thomas and Charles looked scared and despondent. My heart ached for them; I wanted them to know that I was all right.

I looked at Sarah, who was beckoning me to come with her. I looked back at my family. I felt torn and unsure. I wanted to be with Sarah, but my heart was pulling me back home.

"I want to stay, Mama," I whispered delicately.

Sarah lingered close to me and placed her hands on the sides of my face. She leaned down and stared into my eyes, placed a delicate kiss on my lips and pulled me forward. She wrapped me into her arms, covering me with her white satin nightgown. I felt my mind relax, my body weightless and peaceful. The images began, swarming around my soul. Images and long forgotten memories of my mother's love for me, encasing my heart like a cozy blanket on a wintry night. Images of my mother bathing me delicately as a child, the unconditional love in her eyes and the song in her voice. Images of my mother pushing me on the swing set at the playground, laughing as I squealed to go higher and higher. My mother reading me a bedtime story, her arms wrapped

345

around my small body, easing me into sleep as she kissed my face and ran her fingers through my tangled hair. Blessed memories that I had forgotten, the love and attention I received so young, creating the person I am today.

Sarah released me carefully, her eyes penetrating mine, her unspeaking voice ringing in my ears. "I love you, Lucy. Go now, take care of your family."

My eyes sprung open as I heard the screaming of the ambulance's siren in my ears. Nicholas was there, holding my hand, watching me intently, concern riddled all over his face. He saw my eyes. He smiled.

"Lucy! Lucy! Can you hear me? You're going to be okay. Stay with me, keep your eyes open!" Nicholas leaned over and kissed my lips and cheeks. "You stay with me, you hear? I have plans for us, okay? Lots of plans."

I smiled weakly and closed my eyes carefully, feeling my mother's presence and love throughout my body. I didn't want to lose the memories of her, I didn't want to forget, so I closed my eyes tight. I squeezed Nicholas' hand several times so that he knew that I was with him.

"Lucy, everyone is safe. Kat and Amelia are at the hospital. It's over. Do you hear me? It's over!"

I could hear him. I could smell him as he leaned over me, expressing the great news. I could feel the EMT working on my arm, the pain and discomfort a welcoming feeling that I was still alive and well.

I prayed silently to my mother. "Thank you, Mama. Thank you."

I opened my eyes again slowly and looked into the face of the man who saved my life. "Nicholas, come closer," I whispered.

Nicholas leaned over my face so he could hear me speak.

"Kiss me again," I requested with a sly smile.

Nicholas hovered over me, our eyes locked, our faces inches apart. He bent down and kissed me delicately. He rested his face on mine and breathed heavily, not wanting to remove himself from our intimate moment as he exhaled a huge sigh of relief.

"You scared the hell out of me, little girl," he said as he moved my hair off my forehead and away from my neck.

I closed my eyes again, exhaustion overtaking my mind and body.

"Thank you Nicholas."

My nightmare was over, my mind at rest, my family safe. I felt peace and closure.

I felt loved.

CHAPTER 52

Lucy

I sat at Amelia's bedside, not wanting to disturb her. Her head was wrapped in bandages and I could see the bald spot where they shaved her hair to place the stitches. Her pretty face was bruised and battered.

I watched the baby's heart monitor beep, beep, beep, its constant rhythm and noise providing me with peace. I waited for Amelia to open her eyes. She has been in and out of consciousness all day. I've missed her awakening twice already, but she has asked for me every time. I didn't want to disappoint her.

I covered her body with a blanket brought in by my father. It was my mother's blanket. She'd knitted it herself. I was exhausted but relieved that everyone was safe.

I looked down at my bandaged arm. Demetry's dog had bitten and pulled at my arm so viciously that it tore my tendons and muscles and nicked an artery, causing major blood loss. The surgeons where able to save my arm from amputation but said that I would have a hard road of rehab ahead of me. I wasn't too concerned about my arm. I knew that it would heal and that I would move on from my physical ailments. Emotionally, though, I was scarred.

Amelia stirred in her bed, wincing slightly from the irritation of all the wires attached to her body. I moved my chair closer to her bedside, holding on to her hand tightly.

"Tommy," she whispered.

"It's Lucy, Amelia. I'm here with you," I said. "Thomas went home to shower, but he will be back soon," I added to comfort her.

My brother hasn't left her side for a second. I promised him that I would sit with her until he returned. He has been punishing himself with guilt and remorse for days. I tried to reassure him that he wasn't to blame for Amelia's attack. It didn't matter to him. He believed that he should have been with her. He wished he'd never left her. I didn't argue with him. I knew that she would be all right and that she would eventually heal, like I would.

"Lucy." Amelia cried softly as she reached for me. I stood and leaned over her face and kissed her cheeks. Tears of relief fell from Amelia's eyes as I gently tried to hug her.

"I'm sorry, Amelia. I'm sorry this happened to you."

Amelia moved her arm slowly to her head. "They shaved my hair," she whispered with a frown.

"It will grow back, I promise."

"Your arm, is it okay?" she asked.

"It's sore, but I'll live."

"That son of a bitch," Amelia stated.

I started to laugh. It was always shocking to hear such harsh words coming out of her delicate mouth.

"It's over now, Amelia. No one can hurt us now."

"Kathryn, she saved me," Amelia said gratefully, "and the baby."

"I know, Amelia. I know." I watched Amelia close her eyes again.

A nurse came into the room to check on her vitals. She looked at me with compassion in her eyes. "How are our patients today?"

"I'm fine, ma'am. Amelia just woke, but I think she fell asleep again."

The nurse looked over at Amelia, lying in her bed.

"She'll be more alert tomorrow. She's doing well considering what she went through and it's only been a few days. She lost a lot of blood and it took over fifty stitches to close that wound on her head." She smiled softly. "She's lucky to be alive, she's lucky she made it to the hospital in time." The nurse walked around and glanced over Amelia's monitors. "There's a man waiting for you in your room, Lucy. He's been there for some time."

I looked up at the nurse, questioning.

"Would you like me to walk you back to your room?"

"No, thank you. I think I'll stay here until Tommy returns. Whoever is waiting for me can wait some more." I knew that it was Jack. He came every day to check in on me. We haven't spoken yet; I'm not sure how I feel.

Nicholas left for Boston yesterday. He escorted Charles and Kat back to their apartment and helped them remove their personal items. They needed to complete some paperwork on Charles and close the case for good. He said he was looking forward to getting back to work. I assured him that I would be fine. My family was here with me, constantly supporting me, checking in on me. Besides, I was being released from the hospital tomorrow. There was no reason for Nicholas to stick around to watch me heal. He has done more than enough for me. I was grateful to him.

I sat in the hospital room and looked around at all the equipment and devices. I thought about my mother. An overwhelming sadness filled my soul as I thought about our traumatic summer. I had such high hopes for a fun-filled summer. This obviously wasn't the case.

I heard Thomas coming down the hallway. He stopped to speak to the head nurse regarding Amelia's current condition. He swept into the room, eager to check on her and to hear the baby's heartbeat.

"Thank you, Lucy. Thank you for sitting with her."

"She woke up. I was able to speak with her. She swore at me." I laughed.

Thomas smiled. "I love it when she swears. It gives me hope that she'll fight through this and pull out swinging."

I stood from my chair. "She'll definitely pull through this, Tommy. I'm convinced." I leaned over and kissed my brother on his head. "I'm going back to my room now. I'm tired."

"Okay. Thanks again."

I walked back down the hallway slowly. I thought about Jack. I wished things weren't so complicated. I knew he was regretful. He wouldn't be here if he wasn't sorry, or if he didn't care about me. I didn't know if I could forgive him. I didn't know how to work this out, living so far apart. It seemed impossible.

I stopped in front of my hospital room and glanced into the doorway. I could see Jack sitting in a chair by the window. He held his cowboy hat in his hands, nervously turning it around and around. I could feel my chest constrict and my belly start to flutter. I was nervous. My hands shook as I placed them on the door to open it. I wanted to run to him and cry like a baby. I wanted to forget everything once again and be lost in his arms. I wiped the tears that gathered in my eyes as I tried to gather myself. I knew we were both hurting. I knew I was scared.

What if he was here to say goodbye? As angry as I was at him, I didn't want him to leave Connecticut. I wanted him to change his mind, declare his love and stay with me. My heart was pounding in my ears; sudden desperation was constricting my soul. I needed to let go of the anger; I needed to be vulnerable, I needed to take a chance.

I opened the door to the room. Jack stood as I entered, eager to help me to my bed.

"Hey Jack," I said softly as I moved across the room. Jack stared into my face as he held my arm carefully. His eyes were serious and determined. His touch was delicate and gentle. His concern was genuine.

"How are you feeling, Luce?" he asked as he lingered over my bed, watching me settle into my sheets.

"Tired." I sat back in my bed, thinking of the words I wanted to say.

Jack sat with his hands together on the chair, staring at me, considering his own words carefully. I was terrified he was here to say goodbye. I sat in my bed, my heart tearing apart, not wanting this to end. I wanted to beg him to stay; my life would never be the same without him. He was all I needed.

The phone began to ring. I looked over at the receiver. I knew that it was Nicholas. He was the only one who called this line. I felt torn, but I didn't want to answer it. I knew what I wanted.

"Please don't answer that," Jack said softly.

I glanced up into his face.

Jack quickly stood and moved over to my bedside, his body and face inches away from mine.

"I made a terrible mistake, Lucy."

I blinked several times, trying to fight back the tears that wanted to escape my eyes. I stared at Jack; unable to speak knowing my voice would crack if I did.

"I love you, Lucy. Please, you need to forgive me. I can't imagine my life without you."

Jack lowered his head and reached for my injured arm. He held onto my fingers carefully, not wanting to hurt me. I sat quietly and watched his face as he examined my injury.

"I should have been here. This should have never happened."

"What about my family, Jack? I can't leave them, not now."

"I'm not leaving you, Lucy. I will stay here. I will wait for you."

Jack looked up into my eyes. He leaned in closer to my face and put his hand on my cheek. My heart raced as I felt the heat from his skin soaking into mine. He kissed me. He kissed me like he may never kiss me again. I wrapped my good arm around his neck and held on while he carefully laid me against my pillow. I pulled him into me. I held onto him tight.

He carefully crawled into bed and we lay together. I felt his breath against my neck. I felt his chest rise and fall as he exhaled a sigh of relief. He held me tight. I loved his familiar scent. My thoughts raced back to that night we were alone together. Alone and in love, obsessed with one another. I thought back to that day when his mother died. The lost look in his eyes, the helplessness in his voice. I recognized that look now. He was alone and helpless.

I cried, unable to restrain my emotions any longer. I loved him. I always have, I always will.

357

"I love you, Jack."

CHAPTER 53

Jack

I drove through town as fast as I could, eager to get home. The anticipation was killing me. I drove my old pickup truck past the cornfields, past the feed store, over the hills and around the corners until I reached the farm. I pulled into the driveway quickly and impatiently, creating a cloud of dust as I parked my truck near the front porch. I opened the door and jumped out, greeting my buddy Emmitt as he licked my face and jumped onto my chest.

"Hey boy, how's Mama today?"

The yellow lab wagged his tail and barked as I moved along and approached the farmhouse. I saw her figure behind the screen door as I drew near. She opened the door with a beautiful smile. She stepped out onto the porch and jumped into my arms.

"Hey baby," I said as I held her tight. I placed her down delicately on the porch and kissed her pretty face. "I couldn't wait to come home to you." I smiled down at her. "Are you ready?"

The past two years had been a whirlwind of activity. After Amelia and Thomas' baby was born, Lucy and I decided we couldn't wait for our life to begin. Our wedding was a welcomed event for all involved and especially for Lucy's family. Her sisters were bridesmaids and her father, very proud. Even Detective Nicholas was present. His friendship with Lucy and her family was strong and permanent. He and his new wife were happy to be a part of the celebration.

It had been seven months since we moved back to Indiana now, and we couldn't be happier.

"She's been waiting all morning, Jack," Susie Mae commented from behind.

"I kept thinking, what kind of surprise could this be? You've given me everything I've ever wanted."

"Not everything," I said secretively. "Take my hand, I can hardly wait. We'll be back shortly, Susie!" I yelled into the house.

Susie Mae came to the screen door and winked at me as I helped my wife down the stairs. She smiled knowingly, aware of the great surprise I had in store for Lucy.

"Jack, really, whatever you've done, it's not necessary. You need to stop giving me things. I'm perfectly content!" She smiled. I helped my round, pregnant wife climb into my old pickup. I smiled down at her and kissed her lips.

"That's why I'm so excited. I know you don't need anything, Lucy, but I want to give you everything."

I shut Lucy's door carefully and ran around the truck and jumped into the driver seat, then yelled for Emmitt to jump in the back. The yellow lab eagerly jumped into the bed of the truck and we slowly made our journey out of the driveway. I eased the truck carefully up the long road along side the farm. We passed the cornfields, down around the corner and then slowly up the dirt road toward the top of the property.

I thought about my first trip around the property with Pop so many years before. I thought about how impressed I was with the farm and how safe and secure I felt in my new life. I wanted nothing more than to provide that feeling and security for my own family, for my wife and my unborn child. I felt such pride as I carefully made my way up the bumpy terrain, conscious of Lucy's condition and comfort.

"How come I've never been back here?" Lucy asked as the scenery began to unfold.

"It's a very special place, Lucy. I've been saving it for this moment."

Lucy watched as the farm came in full view, the landscape of the land breathtaking and spectacular.

I stopped my truck just before the peak of the hill. I climbed out and helped my wife down off her seat. Emmitt jumped out and disappeared up over the peak.

"Jack, I don't know what to say. It's absolutely gorgeous." Lucy grabbed my hand as I continued to pull her up the hill.

"There's one more thing, Lucy," I said as I urged her forward.

Lucy began to laugh at my enthusiasm. "I've never seen you so excited," she teased me.

I smiled down at her as I watched her waddle up the hill. My heart was bursting.

"Just a little bit farther," I encouraged. Lucy climbed the last leg of the hill and finally reached the top.

"Pop!" she said, surprised as she laid her eyes on my grandfather and several other men working. They all stopped and looked at her with affection. "What's going on?" she asked as Pop approached her with a smile.

"We're building a foundation," he said casually. Lucy looked around her at the men piling granite and concrete, the outline of a square box located perfectly at the top of this small mountain, overlooking the valley.

I watched her carefully and waited. I waited for it to settle in. Finally, she understood.

"Jack?" she said, shocked.

"It's for our family, Lucy. We are going to live here, in this house."

Lucy stared at me, unable to speak.

"I can't believe it," she said as she approached my grandfather. "Pop, this is amazing!" She grabbed him and kissed his face affectionately. Lucy turned to me and I smiled at her. She jumped into my arms and hugged me tight. She kissed my face a thousand times.

363

"Are you surprised?" I asked.

Lucy nodded her head yes as she buried her face in my shoulder. I held her and swung her around carefully. I put her down on her feet and started to walk her around the property. I pointed to the barns and the meadows and the orchards, talking animatedly while showing her the land, just like Pop did so long ago. I smiled continuously as I walked her around our house.

My life was perfect. I was happy and content in every way imaginable. I sat Lucy down in a chair and watched her as she looked out over the land. I knelt down beside her, taking her hand into mine. She looked down at me with her beautiful smile.

"I love you, Jack," she said.

I reached up and kissed her face. "I love you so much."

Emmitt nuzzled his way into our space and interrupted our special moment.

"I love you too, Emmitt." Lucy laughed as she rubbed his head roughly. She looked at me seriously. "Jack, our family is perfect."

"Our family is right."

We sat and enjoyed the prospects of our new life together.

It was the right family. The family I was meant for....

THE END

Thank You

Dear Reader,

*With great gratitude, I wish to thank you for your time and for reading **My Mother's Gift**.*

I hope that you enjoyed it and encourage you to follow me on facebook.com/SusanBRoara, Amazon's author page Susan B. Roara, and on Goodreads.

I look forward to your reviews and comments.

Thank you!

Susan B. Roara